CHARLES DREW
LIFE-SAVING SCIENTIST

Miles J. Shapiro

RSVP

**RAINTREE
STECK-VAUGHN**
P U B L I S H E R S
The Steck-Vaughn Company

Austin, Texas

Acknowledgments

The publisher would like to thank Edward L. Snyder, M.D., professor and blood bank director at Yale Medical School and Yale-New Haven Hospital for his expert review of the manuscript.

Published by Raintree Steck-Vaughn Publishers, an imprint of Steck-Vaughn Company.

Series created by Blackbirch Graphics
Series Editor: Tanya Lee Stone
Editor: Lisa Clyde Nielsen
Associate Editor: Elizabeth M. Taylor
Production/Design Editor: Calico Harington

Raintree Steck-Vaughn Staff
Editors: Shirley Shalit, Kathy DeVico
Project Manager: Lyda Guz

Library of Congress Cataloging-in-Publication Data

Shapiro, Miles.
    Charles Drew: life-saving scientist / Miles J. Shapiro.
        p.   cm. — (Innovative minds)
    Includes bibliographical references and index.
    Summary: Discusses the brief life of an extraordinary young doctor whose research with blood left us many legacies.
    ISBN 0-8172-4403-4
    1. Drew, Charles Richard, 1904--1950—Juvenile literature. 2. Surgeons—United States—Biography—Juvenile literature. 3. Afro-American surgeons—United States—Biography—Juvenile literature. 4. Blood banks—United States—Biography—Juvenile literature. [1. Drew, Charles Richard, 1904-1950. 2. Physicians. 3. Afro-Americans—Biography.]   I. Title. II. Series.
RD27.35.D74S53   1997
617'.092—dc20
[B]   96-20312
                                                                            CIP
                                                                            AC

Printed in the United States of America
1 2 3 4 5 6 7 8 9 0   LB 00 99 98 97 96

TABLE OF CONTENTS

Dr. Charles Drew's research in blood led to
the establishment of blood banks worldwide.

Among
The
Giants

In 1940, Charles Richard Drew, M.D., was only 36 years old, but he had already made a name for himself in the medical community. One day that year, blood scientists from all over the world gathered in the same room with Drew in New York City. Alexis Carrel, who had won a Nobel Prize in Physiology or Medicine in 1912, occupied a chair. So did Karl Landsteiner, the 1930 winner of the same prestigious award and the man who had developed blood-typing. John Scudder, a doctor with whom Drew was conducting research at Columbia Presbyterian Hospital and the person who had called him to the meeting, was also there. Joining the four men were experts in blood research from the French Air Force, the U.S. Army, the Rockefeller Foundation,

The Components of Blood

Blood is the fluid that circulates through the veins, arteries, capillaries, and the heart, all of which make up the circulatory system. One of the functions of blood is to carry oxygen and nutrients to the cells of the body. It travels in one direction to do this. Its other function is to remove waste materials and carbon dioxide. It travels in another direction to do so. Blood is made up of four parts: red blood cells, white blood cells, platelets, and plasma.

Red blood cells are the disk-shaped particles in blood that carry hemoglobin. Hemoglobin is the iron-bearing protein in the red blood cells, carrying oxygen from our lungs to the rest of the body. The hemoglobin is also responsible for removing the carbon dioxide waste that results from the process of the body's using oxygen and nutrients, a process called metabolism. Red blood cells determine which type of blood a human being has. As Karl Landsteiner discovered in 1901, there are four basic human blood types: A, B, AB, and O.

White blood cells are actually colorless cells that help the human body fight off infections. The three types of white blood cells are monocytes, granulocytes, and lymphocytes. Some white blood cells act like garbage collectors by surrounding and taking away foreign

the National Research Council, and the Academy of Medicine, along with representatives of large pharmaceutical firms.

At that very moment across the Atlantic Ocean, World War II was raging in Europe. Adolf Hitler, the leader of Germany, had unleashed his attack on France. Germany had waged ferocious battles in Europe. Thousands of people, both military and civilian, had been wounded, and the need for blood was becoming urgent, especially in France. It was for this reason that the Blood Transfusion Betterment

particles, such as bacteria, and destroying them. Other white blood cells produce antibodies, which are the blood's defense against specific bacteria. Still others just destroy dead cells.

Platelets are the part of the blood that are small, flat disks that aid in the clotting. If you are bleeding from a cut, for example, your blood begins to clot, you stop bleeding, and a scab forms.

Plasma is the liquid part of blood. Although it is made up mostly of water, it also contains nutrients and hormones. It carries around the three other components of blood: the red blood cells, white blood cells, and platelets.

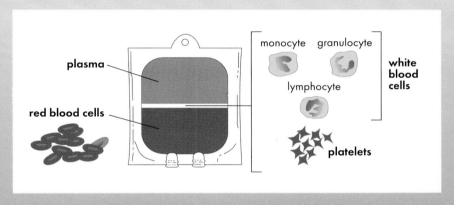

Association now met: to discuss ways to address the problems posed by this brutal war.

Scudder had told Drew just a few hours earlier that an emergency meeting had been called by the Blood Transfusion Betterment Association. Drew was ready. He was still fairly young for a doctor. He was not yet sure why his presence at the important meeting was requested. Only after he and Scudder entered the room where all the greatest blood scientists in the world were assembled did Charles

Drew understand. He had now been invited to join an elite group of doctors in the crucial effort of blood research.

Carrel spoke first, explaining that the situation in Europe was grave. In France, the need for blood was already acute and would become even more so very soon.

One doctor after another offered suggestions about how they might establish a blood bank in France in a very short period of time. Each suggestion, however, proved inadequate to meet the demands of this frightening situation.

John Bush, head of the Blood Transfusion Betterment Association, explained that Scudder and Drew had been carrying out experiments at Presbyterian Hospital. These were funded through an association grant.

Scudder then asked Drew to tell the group about his work. Drew explained his recent discoveries, which concerned plasma transfusions and the establishment of blood banks. The scientists sat quietly and listened to the brilliant doctor, who had that year become the first African American to be awarded the prestigious degree of Doctor of Science in Medicine.

Charles Drew's doctoral thesis had been a 245-page paper entitled *Banked Blood*. In it, Drew explained how blood had been collected, stored, and dispersed up until 1940. He also discussed the discoveries he had made in the laboratories of Columbia Presbyterian Hospital, where he performed most of his blood research. In fact, Drew was perhaps the leading expert in the Western world on blood and plasma transfusion. The experts that were gathered in that room took his ideas very seriously.

The Blood Transfusion Betterment Association had had every intention of using Drew's methods for establishing a blood bank in France, but before they could, that country fell to Germany. There was no longer an immediate need to establish a blood bank because the bloodshed had stopped.

Peace, however, would be brief. In July 1940, Hitler informed his generals and military advisors that he would invade England. Only a month later, German planes attacked British airfields.

On September 7, 1940, life in London changed forever. Almost 320 German bomber planes dropped bomb after bomb on England's capital city. Over the course of 24 hours, 842 Londoners were killed. German radio announced that London was "a sea of flames."

Attacks like this one occurred every night for the next four weeks. Thousands of tons of bombs were dropped, and hundreds of Londoners died or were injured. Many of those

Officials searched through the wreckage of a bombed-out residential area in northwest London after a German raid in the early 1940s.

who survived badly needed blood. Unfortunately, Britain did not have a very large blood-bank system.

The director of England's Army Blood Transfusion Service, John Beattie, was responsible for obtaining blood for the English who had been wounded in the bombings. Beattie requested that a meeting of America's Blood Transfusion Betterment Association be held to address this issue. After several meetings, the Americans established Blood for Britain, a program set up to transport blood from the United States to England for the wounded. Beattie then sent the following telegram to the Americans: "Uniform standards for all blood banks of utmost importance. Suggest you appoint overall director if program is to continue. Suggest Charles R. Drew if available."

Beattie was in a position to know more about Drew's qualifications than anyone. He had been Drew's professor at McGill University's medical school in Montreal, Canada, and Drew had been Beattie's brightest student. The teacher, however, now needed the student's help. He wanted Drew to take charge of the single most significant blood-collection project in history.

He also knew that Drew would be eager to help Beattie, who was one of the many wonderful and devoted teachers who had touched his life. Beattie was right.

At Home in the Nation's Capital

Richard Drew, Charles Richard Drew's father, was a carpet layer for the Moses Furniture Company and the financial secretary of the local branch of the Carpet, Linoleum, and Soft Tile-Layers Union. Charles's mother, Nora Burrell Drew, was a graduate of the Washington Miner Normal Teachers College. She would eventually leave her job as a teacher to take care of her children. Richard and Nora moved in with his parents in a house situated on Twenty-first Street, in Washington, D.C.

Charles Richard Drew as a baby about six months old

Charles was born on June 3, 1904. He was the first of five Drew children; three sisters (Elsie, Nora, and Eva) and one brother (Joseph) followed. Theirs was a racially mixed community called Foggy Bottom, so named because of the dense fog that would roll into the neighborhood from the Potomac River in the mornings. It was a pleasant, working-class neighborhood not far from the White House. But as the family grew bigger, the house seemed to grow smaller.

In time, the family moved just a few blocks away to E Street, where Nora's parents lived. The house was a big, rambling structure just right for a set of grandparents and the growing Drew family.

Life in early twentieth-century Washington, D.C., was good. For 100 years, the city had been one of the few cities in the South to welcome blacks. Even though black people and white people were not allowed to mingle in most settings, most African Americans in Washington were able to pursue their lives without interference from the harsh prejudicial attitudes prevalent at that time. This atmosphere of tolerance resulted in a firmly established black middle class.

It was in this kind of setting that the Drew family lived when Charlie was a child. His first all-black elementary school was called Briggs Elementary. He transferred from Briggs in the fifth grade to Stevens Elementary. Already it was quite clear that Charlie was a smart child. Not only did he excel in the classroom, but he used his intelligence to earn money outside of school.

Charlie's family was not wealthy. His father insisted that he get a job after school to help out with the family's finances. Charlie chose to sell newspapers. He was ambitious and sold many different newspapers, among them the *Washington Star*, the *Herald*, and the *Post*. Each afternoon, he and his younger brother, Joseph, would stand outside the various government buildings and sell papers to the men and women leaving work.

In a short period of time, Charlie had so many papers to sell that he and his brother rounded up six other boys to help sell them. Utilizing his organizational skills, Charlie arranged for at least one boy to be outside each large government building in the city. Within a few months, Charlie was earning $150 per month, an extremely large sum for a preteen in the early 1900s.

Charlie loved to go swimming with his father in the Potomac River at the end of G Street. Richard taught Charlie and Joseph to swim by having them jump off the gravel barges tied up along the waterfront. Because African Americans were not admitted to public swimming pools, the Drew boys spent a good portion of their summer right there at the end of G Street, splashing in the Potomac.

As a young boy in Washington, D.C., Drew sold newspapers in front of federal buildings such as the Department of State, seen here as it was in the early 1900s.

In 1912, the Young Men's Christian Association opened a gymnasium and pool for African Americans on Twelfth Street. It was not far from Charlie's house. Soon thereafter two other pools opened, even nearer to the Drew home. It was at one of these pools that Charlie discovered organized sports and competition.

The head lifeguard at one of the pools noticed Charlie's exceptional swimming ability. Even though Charlie was just eight years old, the lifeguard suggested that the boy enter races to be held on the Fourth of July.

As it is today, the Fourth was a special day in the nation's capital. On Independence Day in 1912, Howard Taft, the President of the United States, made a speech on the White House lawn. He was trying to halt the campaign of his political opponent, Teddy Roosevelt. The city was charged with excitement.

Charlie felt a different excitement, though—that of competition. He had often challenged others at the river, raced, and won. But this was different. This was official—with a starter's gun, swimming lanes, and a cheering crowd. As Charlie, his brother, and dozens of others headed for the pool, they paused to listen to a band play in the parade. While they waited for their race to begin, though, Charlie was so excited that he could barely sit still.

Finally, it was his turn. When the gun for his first race went off, Charlie shot into the water. He stroked as hard as he could and reached the other side. He turned and headed back. When he got there, he lifted his head out of the water and looked back. He saw that the boy in second place was only just then starting his second lap. When Charlie returned home to Foggy Bottom, he had four medals dangling from his neck. These awards marked the beginning of his life in athletic competition.

As Charlie approached his final year of elementary school, he turned over his lucrative paper-selling business to his brother and took up hand-delivering mail for a nearby post office. He had decided to devote more of his time to sports.

After four years of winning contests—Charlie also played on the Stevens Elementary School championship baseball and basketball teams for three years—it was time to head on to high school. He looked forward not only to the academic challenge, but, particularly, to the athletic challenge. Charlie

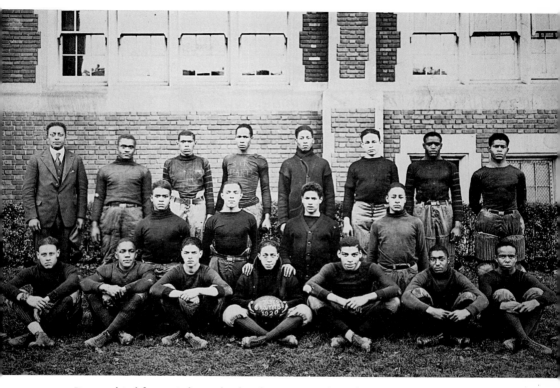

Drew, third from right in the back row, stands with his
championship high school football team in 1920.

would attend Paul Laurence Dunbar High School, which
was, at the time, the finest African-American high school
in the United States. (At one time called the M Street School,
it was renamed to honor the brilliant young poet Paul
Dunbar, who had died in 1906.)

Dunbar was a school with a great academic tradition.
Most of its graduates went on to college, which was unusual for African Americans at this time. As a student, Charlie
was slightly above average, although he excelled at his
science and math courses. As an athlete, however, he was
truly outstanding.

Charlie's academic and athletic interests may have taken center stage at this time, but by no means did his parents neglect another aspect of his upbringing: his spiritual life. At the Nineteenth Street Baptist Church, the Reverend Walter Brooks preached fiery sermons while the Drew children sat as still as they could. The Reverend's instruction to strive to help the community was a powerful message that the family heard clearly. Charlie's mother was a deaconess. His father sang in the choir, along with Charlie and his sisters and brother. The Drew children received religious instruction and took in the moral lessons offered by the Reverend Brooks. They learned about the Bible and about Presbyterian beliefs. They learned about how they were supposed to behave not just in church but in every aspect of their lives. These lessons, about doing what is right for all, are those that Charles Drew learned, and taught, best.

When Charlie entered high school, his world changed. While he quickly established himself as a competent student, after classes he was a star. On the football field, the basketball court, the track field, and the baseball diamond Charles Drew became one of the greatest athletes in Dunbar High School history. He lettered in all four sports in both his junior and his senior years, when he received the E. Walker Memorial Medal for being the best all-around athlete in the high school.

His classmates dubbed him Best Athlete, Most Popular, and Student Who Has Done Most for the School. These accomplishments were obviously outstanding, but if one understands the circumstances under which he achieved all this, they are even more so. When Charlie was in tenth grade, his sister Elsie became very ill. She had contracted pulmonary tuberculosis, a disease of the lungs that was more common in the early 1900s than it is today. Gradually, she became increasingly ill and died. This was an enormous loss for the Drew family.

The tragedy served to strengthen Charlie's desire to make the most of his life through excellence. He insisted on continuing his education at Dunbar even though his family had moved across the Potomac River to Alexandria, Virginia. With the loss of his sister ever present in his mind, Charlie commuted to school every day. Despite his grief—and, perhaps in part because of it—he continued to do well in school and dominated his fellow students on the sports fields.

COLLEGIATE
STARDOM

Drew's overall excellence resulted in his winning a scholarship from Amherst College, in Massachusetts. At Amherst, he continued his athletic career and, of course, his studies. Since he needed money to pay for books and living expenses, he also got a job as a waiter. He kept that job throughout his four years of college.

During Drew's first year at Amherst, he spent most of his energies on sports. As a result, he did not do well in his studies. This caught the attention of the dean of the school, who called Drew into his office to discuss the situation. The dean suggested that he give up sports until he was able to cope with his schoolwork. Drew thought it over. Typically, he decided to treat the problem as a challenge. He would keep on playing sports but at the same time work much harder at his studies.

As Drew began to leave the office, the dean offered this note of warning: "Negro athletes are a dime a dozen." He meant that while Drew might excel in sports, this would not be a remarkable achievement. But if he, a black man, were to excel in school and, eventually, in his profession, it would be not only a personal success but one that could benefit the entire African-American community.

This made an impression on the young man. Since the death of his sister, Drew had thought that he might like to become a doctor and help sick children like Elsie. He now decided to enter Amherst's premedicine program. Drew continued to star in sports, but he began to do much better academically as well.

In a football game during his junior year, Drew was injured when a spike on an opponent's shoe cut his thigh. The injury proved to be rather serious. When the wound became infected, he had to go to the hospital.

His recovery took an entire week. One of the doctors knew that Drew was a premed student and tried to encourage him. He allowed the young man to come along as he made his rounds to look in on the other patients. One of these patients had just had his appendix taken out. As the doctor pulled back the clean, white hospital sheet, Drew noticed that a tube was inserted into the patient's stomach. The tube was also pinned to the skin of the stomach so that it would not slip into the incision. The sight of this seemingly crude medical procedure captivated him. At that moment, he made a transition from an athlete who was a premed student to a premed student who happened to be an athlete.

LEGALLY SEPARATE

Throughout Charles Drew's life, segregation—the legal separation of African Americans from the rest of the people in America—existed in many parts of the United States.

Segregation was the offspring of slavery in the United States. From the mid-1600s until the 1860s black people had been forced into servitude. Although the slave trade had nearly disappeared in the

For many decades after the end of slavery in the United States, African Americans were legally restricted from having many of the privileges other Americans enjoyed. Often separate, or segregated, places were created for whites and blacks.

North by 1800, it had not disappeared in the South. Southerners relied on slave labor to keep their large plantations—where crops such as cotton and sugar were grown—running. Northerners, however, had an economy that was not so reliant on farming.

Tension between supporters of slavery and their opponents came to a head in 1861, with the bombardment of a Northern fort. The North and South engaged in a bitter war, the Civil War, which the North won. Subsequently, in 1865, the Thirteenth Amendment to the Constitution was passed, declaring that slavery was illegal. The Fourteenth Amendment, passed in 1868, said that all people born in the United States were citizens and, thus, were free. The Fifteenth Amendment, passed in 1870, allowed all male citizens, regardless of race or color, to vote. (Women would not be given the vote for another 50 years, until the Nineteenth Amendment was passed in 1920.)

The South resented losing the war. In an attempt to create a legal system that kept things as they had always been before, the South instituted segregation. Southern states passed laws called Jim Crow laws. According to these laws, blacks were not permitted to use the same restrooms as whites. They were not allowed to remain in a seat on a bus or other mode of public transportation if a white person wanted that seat. They sat in the back of the bus or in special sections on trains. Blacks were restricted from most activities and places of entertainment that whites could enjoy.

Although legally African Americans had the right to vote, individual Southern states passed laws that made it impossible for most blacks to exercise their right. What resulted were two entirely different societies in the South, one for whites and one for blacks.

This unfair system continued until 1954, when the U.S. Supreme Court ruled that school systems that kept children of different races separate were illegal. The famous case that prompted the Supreme Court's decision was called *Brown v. Board of Education of Topeka* (Kansas), and it was only the beginning of the end of segregation. The fact that this milestone was reached after Charles Drew's life was already over makes his achievements in the face of prejudice and hatred even more outstanding.

Even so, Drew continued to excel in athletics. In football, he dominated the competition. During the 1925 championship game against Wesleyan University, he returned a kickoff for a touchdown and launched a 35-yard touchdown pass with time running out to win the biggest game of the year. "A storybook ending to a game if ever there was one," recalled fellow teammate Monty Cobb.

Drew's athletic talents stood out during his years at Amherst College.

Charles Drew

Drew won the Thomas W. Ashley Memorial Trophy for Most Valuable Player on the Amherst College football team in both his junior and senior year. In addition, he received the honorable-mention all-American award those same two years for playing the halfback position.

Drew was also a gifted sprinter and trackman. He performed the 120-yard high hurdles, for which he won the National Championship and set a school record of 15.2 seconds. He was captain of the team and won the Howard Hill Mossman Cup, an award for "bringing the greatest honors in athletics" to Amherst in 1926.

Although Charles Drew enjoyed nearly perfect success in sports, he did face some problems. Most of these had to do with the fact that he was African American. When he was tackled during a football game, for example, some of his white opponents would call him racist names. Drew would get so angry that, with his light complexion and freckles, he would turn bright red. His teammates, who correctly assumed that he was furious, nicknamed him Big Red. No matter how angry he was, though, he never fought with anyone who insulted him. He just tried harder to win the football game. Much later his wife would recall, "He already had decided our people [African Americans] could make more progress by 'doing and showing' than by violent demonstration."

The most overt instance of racial prejudice Drew had encountered occurred while he was in his junior year of college. The Amherst track team had traveled to Providence, Rhode Island, to face the Brown University team. After the meet, the team returned to the Narragansett Hotel for a banquet. Once there, they found out that the hotel did not allow black people into the building. No other hotel would take in the entire team on such short notice. So Drew and fellow African-American athletes Bill Hastie and Monty Cobb went back to the university commons to eat their dinner. Upset, the trio sat silently on the bus ride back to Amherst.

A similar incident occurred during Drew's senior year of college. Upon arriving in Boston, Massachusetts, the coach, Tuss McLaughry, discovered that the hotel would not allow the black team members to stay overnight. McLaughry immediately gathered his team and ordered everyone to leave while the desk clerk complained, "What about these reservations? We've been holding these rooms! You can't just walk out like this!" Coach McLaughry's reply was short: "You just watch, mister!"

McLaughry liked Drew very much and thought very highly of him both as a student and an athlete. Indeed, he was so impressed with the young man that more than 25 years later, after an extremely successful career of coaching, he wrote an article about Charles Drew. Entitled "The Best Player I Ever Coached," it was published in the *Saturday Evening Post*. McLaughry said in the article that "as a football player, Drew was great. He could have played regular on any team in the country, both in his era and anytime since."

Drew finished college cloaked in awards and honors. He had every intention of attending medical school. Judging by his academic and athletic record, he should have had no problem gaining acceptance into any medical school in the country. Unfortunately, Drew was not able to attend. His brother, Joseph, had just begun his college studies at Howard University. His youngest sibling, Eva, had been born just the year before. There was still a mortgage to pay on the house in Virginia. Charles Drew's father could not

Drew (right) had to postpone his medical studies after graduation from college. His father (middle) had other financial obligations, such as his brother Joseph's (left) college tuition.

work any harder or longer to pay for all the things his family needed. There was simply not enough money to pay for medical school.

Coaching...and Waiting

Drew was not angry about this delay. On the contrary, he remembered his mother telling him that his father had gone into debt to pay for Charles's college education. Medical school looked like a financial impossibility for now. Instead, Drew took a job as a coach, teacher, and athletic director at Morgan College, now called Morgan State University, in Baltimore, Maryland.

Drew had every intention of working for just a few years, saving his money, and then attending the medical school of Howard University. He told the president of Morgan College about his plans, explaining that he wanted to go to Howard, at the time the most prestigious black university in the country. Along with Meharry Medical School, in Tennessee, Howard turned out nearly 80 percent of all the African-American doctors in the entire country. In addition, Howard was in Washington, D.C., his hometown. Although he didn't know it then, Drew would find the trip home to Washington longer and more circuitous than anything he had ever expected.

The Making
of a
Scientist

During the time between finishing college and earning enough money for medical school, Charles Drew devoted himself to Morgan College's athletics department. While this period of Drew's life might be considered a detour, it is during this time that he developed many of the skills that made him one of the most important figures in modern medical science.

At Morgan College, Drew got a chance to make use of some of his talents and abilities that he would later draw on as a scientist and a teacher of surgeons. He organized what was once a very poor football team into a very competitive one. The team had never beaten the Howard University

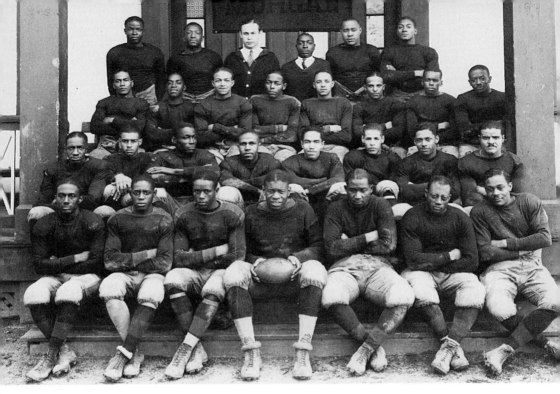

Drew coached and taught at Morgan College in order to earn money for medical school. He is seen here (third from left, top row) with Morgan's football team.

team. In fact, the team had never scored a single touchdown against Howard. When Drew arrived, his first task was to persuade his best athlete, Daniel "Pinky" Clark, to stay at Morgan and not transfer to a school with better and more established sports teams.

Drew encouraged his team to try harder. He organized them into a tight, hardworking unit. He had a knack for succeeding in the face of challenging situations. To do so, he used his two best skills: the ability to inspire others to perform the difficult task before them, and the ability to organize that task and everybody involved to make it easier. He did this at Morgan, and the results were clear. The group of young men became a team geared toward a unified goal. For the first time in a long while, Morgan began to win a few games.

And they scored a touchdown against Howard, even though, in the end, they lost the game.

That year, Drew coached the football and basketball teams and also taught science, chemistry, and biology. His salary was small; $1,500 a year, plus room and board. Still, it was enough to allow him to start saving some money to attend medical school at Howard University.

Drew worked at a local pool during the summers to supplement his income.

Drew returned home to Washington, D.C., for the summer, where he worked as the head lifeguard at a neighborhood swimming pool. His younger brother, Joe, was also a lifeguard there. In the fall, he returned to Morgan and resumed teaching and coaching. He also began applying to medical school.

Drew's performance as a team coach, athletic director, and teacher was excellent. Everyone was extremely pleased with the job he was doing, and they wanted him to continue. The football team was an even bigger success in Drew's second year. The students enjoyed having a football team that they could be proud of.

The heads of Morgan College did not want Drew to leave the school. Following a meeting with the faculty in 1928, the president, Dr. Spencer, and the registrar, Ed Wilson, pleaded with him to stay at Morgan. They argued that, for the first time, the football team's success had generated interest from the alumni. The school was now receiving money donations from the alumni, because they were so proud of the team's success. They realized how valuable Drew was to the college. Spencer said, "Ed and I want you, the regents want you, the alumni want you, and, not least, the student body wants you."

It was hard to do, but Drew turned them down. He had decided what he wanted to do with his future. He could not be convinced otherwise. "I'm afraid not," Drew said, refusing their offer of a quite substantial pay raise. "I guess I'm bullheaded, but I've decided on medicine and not coaching as a career."

Wilson replied, "None of us expected you to change your mind, Charlie, but we had to try."

In May, Drew sent in his application to Howard University's medical school. Then he waited confidently for a reply.

HOWARD'S LOSS IS CANADA'S GAIN

When Drew heard from the university, he was crushed: Howard had turned him down for lack of two English credits—an academic technicality. Drew was angry, and he took the letter into Wilson's office. He showed Wilson the letter and said that he wanted him to send copies of his Amherst transcript to other schools.

Wilson could see that Drew was not going to give up easily. The two of them sat down together and completed Drew's applications to a handful of medical schools around the country and in Canada.

Although Drew recovered from the rejection of his application by Howard University, he remained disappointed. He swore to his brother Joe that he would someday run the place that had rejected him.

Drew soon heard from the other medical schools, and all of them found his college grades to be excellent. Howard, on the other hand, contacted him to offer him a coaching position—a request that hurt his pride. Still disappointed, he sifted through his acceptance letters, which had come from Harvard as well as other schools.

Drew finally selected McGill University, in Montreal, Canada. His decision was based on his past experiences with discrimination, even in the supposedly nonracist North. He had not forgotten the humiliation of having to eat in the Brown University cafeteria while his white teammates enjoyed their meal at the Narraganset Hotel. Drew guessed that classmates and faculty members might treat him more fairly were he to attend school in Canada.

McGill turned out to be an excellent choice. It was a place where he would make important connections that would have a dramatic impact on his medical career.

Before attending medical school, Drew finished out the school year at Morgan College and returned to his lifeguard job in Washington, D.C. After that second summer of hard work and saving, he had enough money to begin at McGill.

Drew attended McGill University, which rests on one
of the slopes of Mount Royal in Montreal, Canada.

Charles Drew

In Montreal, Drew immediately found employment as a waiter. He needed the money to maintain even the lowest standard of living while in medical school. During his first year, he often had to pass up the opportunity to socialize with his friends. They received money from home to pay for tickets to plays or for other kinds of entertainment. Drew did not have anything left over after paying rent for his room and for his meals.

Furthermore, he was lonely and wrote: "Here I am: a stranger amongst strangers in a strange land, broke, busted, almost disgusted, doing my family no good, myself little that is now demonstrable. I must go on somehow—I must finish what I have started."

Drew took the task of medical school quite seriously. In college, his academic record had been mediocre in some ways. In medical school, however, it was excellent. Early on at McGill, his academic record was so strong that he won election to Alpha Omega Alpha, the medical students' honorary scholastic fraternity.

He did not, however, abandon sports. Drew joined the McGill track team. In one meet, he scored an amazing 66 points for his team—a school record. And in his second year, Drew was elected captain of the team. Some speculate that he is the only man to have been elected captain of a varsity sport at two separate universities.

In Drew's second year, he began to suffer from the strain of academics, sports, and having to be on his feet for long hours as a waiter. He was sure that he would have to quit his waiter job, but he worried that he would also have to quit medical school for lack of funds.

But good fortune touched Drew at just the right moment. A group of his former classmates at Amherst pooled their

Heritage of Success

Charles Drew was an African American who achieved many great things. But, like other important scientists and inventors, his successes were built upon the achievements of others who came before him. Here is a chronology of some of their accomplishments.

1660s Lucas Santomee is regarded as the first black physician in the New World, practicing in what was then called New Amsterdam, now known as New York.

1760s James Derham of New Orleans, Louisiana, is the first black doctor trained in America.

1830s The American Colonization Society, a society committed to resettling blacks in Liberia, on the African continent, arranges the training of a few black doctors.

1847 David Peck is the first black in America to receive a medical degree from a university, Rush Medical College.

1868 Howard Medical College in Washington, D.C., is established as the first medical school for the training of black physicians.

1876 Meharry Medical College, in Nashville, Tennessee, is established to train black physicians.

circa 1900 Three African-American inventors—Granville T. Woods, Lewis H. Latimer, and Elijah McCoy—create a series of new inventions. Woods, awarded dozens of patents—mostly for inventions having to do with the railroads—invents the electromotive train system, the galvanic battery, the ironing table, and the railway telegraph, among other things. Lewis Latimer invents a long-lasting and inexpensive filament for lightbulbs; locking racks for hats, coats, and umbrellas; and other items. McCoy invents devices to provide automatic lubrication for machinery as well as a lawn sprinkler system. (An interesting aside: The phrase "the real McCoy" is derived from Elijah McCoy's name. People did not want items that he did not help to make. They insisted on "the real McCoy.")

1920s By this time, there are more than 30 other all-black medical schools, but 80 percent of black medical-school graduates come from Howard Medical College and Meharry Medical College.

Richard Spikes invents many items, from an automatic gearshift to a multibarrel machine gun and a locking billiard-cue rack.

late 1930s Marian Anderson becomes the first black opera singer to sing at the Metropolitan Opera in New York City. In 1939, Anderson was to sing in Constitution Hall. But because she was black, the Daughters of the American Revolution, who owned the hall, did not allow her to perform. Instead, with the support of the President and First Lady Franklin and Eleanor Roosevelt, she gave a free concert at the Lincoln Memorial. Drew attended the concert and wrote about it in a letter to his future wife.

circa 1940 Charles Drew invents a successful method for the storage of blood plasma.

1947 Jackie Robinson of the Brooklyn Dodgers integrates major league baseball. The entire country takes notice.

This chronology is not complete, but these were Charles Drew's influences—men and women of African heritage who managed, in spite of the prejudice that they may have faced every day, to have a powerful and positive impact on the arts, industry, and institutions of their day. Their contributions continue to enrich the lives of not only other black Americans but of all Americans.

Marian Anderson performed for a large crowd in front of the Lincoln Memorial in Washington, D.C., in 1939.

resources and lent him the money to stay in school. The man behind this plan was Tuss McLaughry, now the track coach at Brown University. McLaughry knew that Drew would be too proud to accept the money as a gift, so he arranged it as a loan.

At the end of his second year, Drew won a $1,000 academic scholarship from the Julius Rosenwald Fund—money that was desperately needed. Two years later he captured the Williams Prize, awarded to the person with the highest score on a test taken only by the top five members of the graduating class.

A Lucky Friendship

One professor who noticed Drew's intelligence and drive was John Beattie, who taught the Introduction to Biology course at McGill. Beattie, like Drew, was not Canadian. He was from England, and the two "outsiders" hit it off. They were an odd-looking pair. Drew was big and broad at the shoulders and through the chest, while Beattie was small and wiry. But they shared a love of sports and a devotion to medicine, and grew to be good friends. Beattie became an important mentor for Drew.

One day when Drew walked by his office at school, Beattie called him inside. Beattie showed him a newspaper article stating that Karl Landsteiner had won the Nobel Prize for work he had done 30 years before on blood-typing. Beattie and Drew discussed the fact that there was no way to know how many people had died during the past three decades because Landsteiner's discoveries had not yet been put to clinical use.

That is not particularly unusual in science, because new ideas are not always easily accepted. Drew observed that, in the seventeenth century, William Harvey was ridiculed when he published his theory on the circulation of blood.

Beattie then told Drew that he had decided to focus more on research than on teaching at this point in his career, as he knew that much research remained to be done in blood. Beattie then turned the conversation toward his student's future. He asked Drew what he was going to do after medical school and suggested that he might give some thought to going into research.

It was a conversation that Drew would recall often. As time went on, he found himself in the library, more and more, studying books on blood research.

Drew would have a long time to think about the possibility of a career in research. Medical school and residency—a period of advanced training—amount to seven years of total devotion to the study of medicine. During those years, a student is exposed to many different aspects of medicine and chooses one area in which he or she wants to specialize. When Drew had that conversation with Beattie, Drew was only in his second year of the seven-year process. No doubt, like many other students, he changed his mind often.

Beattie had told him in the course of the conversation that Drew was very bright, and would make a skilled researcher. For the next five years, this statement rang in Drew's ears. Still, he was also interested in teaching; he wanted to help other African Americans receive medical training. Deciding between teaching and research would be hard.

In his third year of medical school, with the help of a scholarship he won for outstanding academic performance, Drew gave up working outside of school. He concentrated

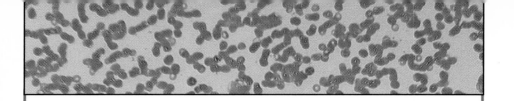

MEDICAL SPECIALTIES

Medical students are exposed to many different categories of medicine throughout their studies. At some point in their schooling, they choose what field they prefer. Some of the general fields of medicine are internal medicine and family practice, but there are many specialties for students to consider. The following is a list of some of the choices available to medical students:

Cardiology The study of the heart and its actions and diseases.

Dermatology A branch of medicine concerned with the skin and its structure, functions, and diseases.

Ear, Nose, and Throat A branch of medicine concerned with the function and diseases of the ears, nose, and throat.

Gerontology The study of aging and problems in the elderly.

Hematology The study of blood and blood-forming organs, like marrow in bones.

Nephrology A branch of medicine concerned with the kidneys.

Neurology The study of the nervous system and its structure, functions, and abnormalities.

Obstetrics and Gynecology A branch of medicine concerned with birth, pregnancy, and female reproduction.

Oncology The study of tumors; especially concerning cancer.

Ophthalmology A branch of medicine dealing with the structure, functions, and diseases of the eye.

Orthopedics The medical specialty of fixing and straightening and correcting deformities in the skeletal system, especially the extremities, the spine, and associated structures, like muscles and ligaments.

Pathology The science and study of the origins and courses of diseases.

Pediatrics A branch of medicine concerned with the developmental care and diseases of children.

Psychiatry A branch of medicine concerned with treating mental disorders.

Surgery A branch of medicine concerned with treating disease, injuries, or deformities through manual or operative procedures.

primarily on medicine and science. He did continue to be on the track team. As was true in high school at Dunbar and in college at Amherst, he was a star athlete. During his fourth year, he even became the team captain.

Drew (first row, center) made time in his schedule to be a member of McGill's track team.

The Making of a Scientist

Residency in Montreal

On a clear, warm day in May 1933, Charles Drew attended the graduation ceremony for medical students at McGill University. He had earned his degrees of Doctor of Medicine and Master of Surgery. Professor Beattie shook Drew's hand in congratulations, and told him that Drew would not soon be forgotten at McGill.

Before beginning his residency in medicine at Montreal General Hospital, however, he returned to Washington, D.C., to see his family. Things were bad there, as they were for some in Montreal. The Great Depression, a time when jobs were hard to find and money was hard to come by, was in full swing. His father had lost his job as a carpet layer, because no one had money to spend on extras like carpeting. During the summer, Drew watched his father sit in the park with nothing to do, and he suffered along with him.

When Drew returned to Montreal and began his residency, he sent as much of his paycheck as he could back home to his family. He could not ignore the fact that his parents had allowed him to pursue his dreams of college and medical school without asking him to help out. During his residency, he worked in internal medicine, pediatrics, oncology, and obstetrics. After that, he concentrated on surgery, which became his specialty.

In the few minutes of spare time he did have, he would visit Beattie in the pathology department. There Beattie had an area set up for determining blood type for transfusions. Transfusions were no longer as dangerous as they had been, but doctors were often confounded as to why some of them went wrong, resulting in patient deaths.

Just as frustrating to doctors was the delay in arranging timely transfusions. If a patient was scheduled to have an operation, the hospital could arrange for donors of the correct blood type to be available. Most of the time, though, patients who needed blood needed it immediately, as a result of some kind of accident.

Witnessing one of these accidents was what pushed Charles Drew to explore the idea of storing blood for use in transfusions. One night, both he and Beattie were on duty when an ambulance brought in a little girl in desperate need of blood. None was available.

The next day, a tired and sad Drew told Beattie that some way must be developed so that blood could be preserved and stored, to be ready for immediate use.

Instantly, Beattie knew what Drew was talking about. He asked if the girl who had been in the wreck had died. Drew nodded, and said that if blood had been immediately available for transfusion, the patient might have lived. They could have typed her blood and gone straight to a blood supply that was already typed and ready to transfuse.

This idea struck a chord with Beattie. He remembered an article from a medical journal he had saved, and he showed it to Drew. It was an article written in 1927 about V. N. Shamov, a Russian doctor who had conducted experiments along the same lines. He had mixed blood from a cadaver with a solution of sodium citrate. Although that prevented the blood from clotting, the red blood cells still kept breaking down. Drew knew that the breakdown of these cells was very dangerous.

While he was reading, Drew was called into surgery as the result of another accident. He scrubbed up and got into surgical gear. Drew took some of the patient's blood and as

Karl Landsteiner's Nobel prize-winning blood-typing
method was put to clinical use by Charles Drew.

Charles Drew

quickly as possible typed it by both the older Landsteiner method and by a newer, more exact one. It was his own blood type, and he promptly rolled up his sleeve and donated blood. It was not the first time he had done this, and it would not be the last time. He would give anything he could—his intelligence, his time, his money, even his blood—to help another person.

He now decided to study the subject of blood transfusions in earnest. He reread the article Beattie had given him about Shamov. He also read an article, published in 1930, about another Russian physician, S. S. Yudin, who had proved Shamov's theory correct.

Drew found these results very promising, but there were many questions yet to be answered. How long does blood last after being treated with the sodium citrate solution? Does adding the sodium citrate change specific qualities of the blood? And most important, how can transfusions be performed quickly enough to save the victims of serious accidents? People who have been in serious accidents often lose a lot of blood. When that happens, they go into shock. Shock is a very dangerous condition, and if not treated, it can lead to death. To treat shock, doctors give blood transfusions. However, if the transfusions are delayed, death often occurs. It is for this reason that the amount of time spent giving a blood transfusion is critical. Drew knew this, and he also knew that he needed answers to his questions in order to save lives.

However, just as Drew began to intensely study blood with Beattie, Beattie decided to return to England. Drew was left alone to ponder the questions of blood and blood transfusions. As there was no central agency or school at which to study this field, everyone involved in this area of

The Making of a Scientist

Charles Drew (third from left, back row) was a
surgical resident at Montreal General. In his spare
time, he began to research blood seriously.

research worked independently. Drew spent a great deal
of time in the McGill University medical library. There he
searched the stacks for all of the studies that had been done
on blood.

Drew was unable to make serious headway in his
research—but only for lack of time. He spent most of his
hours becoming a fine surgeon at Montreal General
Hospital. After a good amount of work, he was certified by
the Canadian National Board of Examiners as a surgical specialist. This was in 1935, and he was just 30 years old.

Amidst the happiness of becoming certified, Drew also confronted tragedy. His father died. Drew immediately headed to Arlington, Virginia, to be with his family. His sister Nora and his brother Joe were now schoolteachers. Eva, just fourteen, was still in high school. All of the Drew children mourned the man about whom their mother used to say, "Don't you ever forget that you were cared for and educated by your father [who worked] on his knees." The funeral was held in the Nineteenth Street Baptist Church, the same church where young Charlie Drew had learned many of his lessons in morality.

It was with those lessons in mind that Charles Drew announced to his family that he was returning to Washington, D.C., for good. Or so he thought.

HOME
AND
AWAY

here was much waiting for Charles Drew in Washington. His mother and brother and sisters could not have been happier to have the eldest child near home. They were a close family, and they needed to gather together and re-establish their family ties—especially since Richard Drew's death. However, Drew had also moved back to Washington, D.C., because there was a job waiting for him.

It was a job he very much wanted, a position as an instructor in pathology at Howard Medical College, Howard University's medical school. Drew felt that he was about to embark on the career he had thought he would pursue when he had spoken with Beattie during medical school. At that time, he had told Beattie that training African Americans for a career in medicine was a frontier in itself—one as valuable and as far-reaching as scientific research.

Drew was received with open arms. The year before, he had contacted his friend from high school and college, W. Montague Cobb, or Monty, who was already a professor of medicine at Howard. Cobb was anxious to put Drew in contact with the impressive new dean of the medical school, Dr. Numa P. G. Adams. It was only after a year of writing letters to Adams that Drew was offered the job at Howard.

The position, while prestigious, did not pay that well, just $150 a month. That was what he had earned by selling newspapers so long ago in elementary school. But making a lot of money was not important to Drew. He could have gone into private practice, but he chose to teach instead.

Freedmen's Hospital, the clinical and teaching facility of Howard, was federally funded, and was not a wealthy institution. Initially, it had been part of the Freedmen's Bureau, a welfare agency founded in 1862 and run by the U.S. government to help freed slaves during and after the Civil War. Many of these people had nowhere else to go when they became ill. Howard University was founded five years later, in 1867. Two years after that, the hospital moved to the Howard University campus. It has been a medical teaching facility ever since.

The hospital and the medical school have a rich tradition of excellence. The first chief of surgery was Robert Reyburn, who held that post until 1875. In 1890, surgeon Daniel Hale Williams performed the first successful heart surgery. Williams reorganized Howard and Freedmen's and, in so doing, created the position of hospital director. He also recruited excellent doctors to fill specialized positions. He

During his career as a doctor and surgeon,
Drew spent many years at Howard University.

even started a nursing school. William A. Warfield directed
the hospital for the next 35 years. Then came Numa Adams.

Strong tradition notwithstanding, Howard's medical students faced tremendous hardship when they left to become
doctors. Once they earned their degrees, most specialized in
a particular field. Howard did not have the facilities to supply all of its students with positions providing training in
their desired specialties. These African-American graduates
were faced with gaining positions at other hospitals, an
endeavor that in the 1930s and 1940s was extremely difficult.
In the South, it was near to impossible.

Drew was keenly aware that he could not determine what would happen to Howard's medical students after they left the nurturing confines of the university. He could insist, however, that while they were at Howard they receive the best possible training that he and the other professors could provide. "It is my belief," he said, "that surgeons can be trained at Howard to be as good as anywhere else." His students confirmed this. One of them, Jack White, recalled that "the last thing he [Drew] said before I left for my residency was that, apart from my ability, he felt that I had developed a very positive self-image, which would stand me well in my relations with other people."

Encouraging students was not Drew's only job. By 1936, he was named assistant in surgery at Howard. He also worked as a surgeon at Freedmen's during this time.

Drew was a valuable surgeon. Howard and Freedmen's Hospital had many black patients. In Washington, D.C., Virginia, and Maryland, African Americans were turned away from most of the other hospitals. Segregation did not exist only in schools. Hospitals throughout the country and especially in the South did not treat black patients in the same manner as white patients. In the South, many hospitals simply refused to treat black patients at all. Sick or injured African-American men, women, and children were forced to travel to black hospitals like Howard or to hospitals that did not have racist policies. Because of this, Freedmen's Hospital was constantly crowded, and Drew was almost always busy.

Also under the Freedmen's Hospital roof labored a particularly eminent doctor named Edward L. Howes, of the Yale School of Medicine. He was there because the Rockefeller Foundation, an organization funded by the wealthy

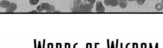

WORDS OF WISDOM

The following are a few inspirational quotes from Dr. Charles Richard Drew. While he was known internationally as "Mr. Blood Bank," others knew him as a dynamic leader and teacher. These are some of his most memorable and enduring thoughts.

On African-American equality and achievement: "Dream high enough and work hard enough and we'll get where we want to go." "Just keep dreaming high, and we'll make the kind of world we want."

To his students at Howard University Medical School: "We're going to turn out surgeons here who will not have to apologize to anybody, anywhere." "If we take care of education, race will take care of itself."

On his students at Howard: "[T]he boys whom we are now helping to train, I believe in time will constitute my greatest contribution to medicine."

On blood and race: "The blood of individual human beings may differ by groupings, but there is absolutely no scientific basis to indicate any difference according to race."

On health care for all: "The enjoyment of the highest attainable standard of health is one of the fundamental rights of every human being without distinction of race, religion, political belief, economic or social condition."

Rockefeller family, had sent him. People at the Foundation understood that black hospitals were in desperate need of help in terms of medical education. Howes was stunned by the conditions at Freedmen's, which were far different from the modern surroundings he had enjoyed at Yale. And Howes was extremely impressed with Charles Drew, whom he considered a gifted surgeon.

Howes had an idea. After discussing it with Adams, he contacted the Rockefeller Foundation on Drew's behalf.

Scientific Opportunity

Adams called Drew to his office, where Howes was waiting. Then they told him the good news. On Howes's recommendation, the Rockefeller Foundation had decided to award Drew a fellowship for advanced training in surgery at Columbia University Medical School, in New York City.

Adams warned that Drew would be working in a research program in addition to his surgery, and the pay was not very impressive. The fellowship would involve blood research with John Scudder, who Drew already knew for his work in treating shock.

At Columbia, Scudder was an assistant professor of clinical surgery who was also busy doing research. The fellowship would enable Drew to do postgraduate work at Columbia. He saw this as a wonderful opportunity to explore another frontier.

Allen Whipple was Columbia's head of the Department of Surgery, and Scudder had discussed the possible difficulties of having a black man on the research team. Although New York was not segregated in the way that the South was—there were no water fountains labeled *white* and *colored*, for example—in fact white people did not mingle with black people, and blacks did not mingle with whites. Whipple and Scudder believed that while there might be some problems, nothing should keep this talented man from working on their team.

When Drew arrived in New York, he knew that this chance represented an important opportunity for the entire African-American community. He was only too aware of his responsibility to perform well in this new position.

In the middle of June 1938, Drew stood outside the Columbia Presbyterian Medical Center, awed by the building's size. Freedmen's Hospital, it seemed, would fit inside the hallways of the great hospital. Drew walked inside Columbia Presbyterian and entered a new world of research and scientific excitement.

He met Scudder for the first time. Their meeting initially was cool but polite. When Drew told Scudder about his

Columbia Presbyterian would be home to Drew for two years while he did postgraduate work in surgery and blood research.

longstanding interest in the study of blood, however, the two men quickly began to warm to each other.

Scudder asked Drew if he had ever heard of a "blood bank." Drew knew of two such "banks." One, which was for civilian use, was set up in Chicago's Cook County Hospital. Bernard Fantus had established an actual blood bank, with people depositing and withdrawing blood. Relatives would donate blood for a member of their family in need of that blood. Drew also knew that during the Spanish Civil War of 1936, F. Duran-Jorda and Norman Bethune had designed a container for storing typed blood. These doctors had also experimented with using dried plasma from old blood in emergencies.

Scudder was excited that someone else was familiar with the history of storing blood and the difficult problem before them: the successful preservation and storage of donated blood for use at a later time.

It was then that Scudder told Drew that Columbia Presbyterian was considering starting up a blood bank. Both men were very happy about the prospect. Drew began studying with a fury he had never before exercised in his academic life. He felt for the first time that he could make a real difference in the field of science. At Howard University and Freedmen's Hospital, he thought he could change the lives of future doctors and, by doing so, change the lives of their patients. At Columbia Presbyterian, however, he was convinced he might change the history of medical science.

Drew's excitement found an audience in Scudder. Impressed with the young doctor's work, he had Drew move into Scudder's own office so that they might work more closely together.

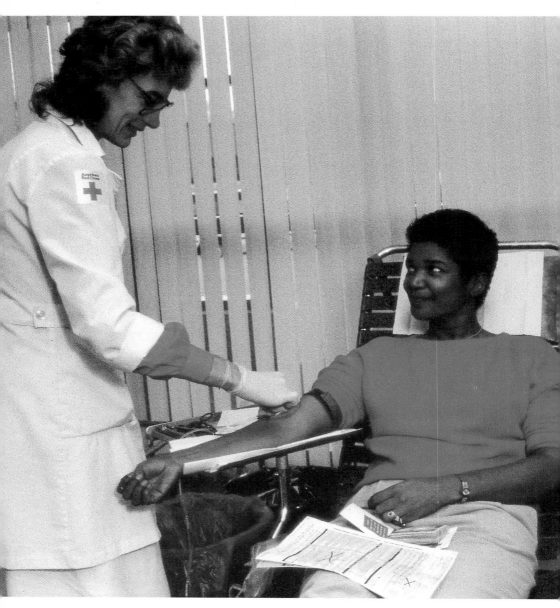

When Drew began working with John Scudder in the late 1930s, blood banks were practically unheard of. Today, the American Red Cross receives blood for its banks from volunteers like this woman (above right), who is shown giving a donation.

Charles Drew

Blood Research

Drew began a systematic collection of all the material that had been written on the storage of blood. He gathered virtually everything there was to be read in the medical library about blood. He started with a study of William Harvey's work on circulation of blood in the body. The theory of circulation implied that blood travels in a circular motion. Blood is pumped from the heart to the lungs. It then travels from the lungs back to the heart. From there it goes to the cells throughout the body, and from the cells back to the heart to start the process again.

William Harvey demonstrates how blood circulates throughout the body. His theory replaced the belief that blood in the body was supplied by the liver and the heart.

Then Drew read the work of scientist Marcello Malpighi, who, in the late seventeenth century, was the first to identify the capillaries. Capillaries carry blood from the arteries to the veins. Arteries are the tubes in the body that carry blood that still contains oxygen, and veins are the tubes that carry blood that has used up its oxygen.

Following Malpighi's discovery, there was much scientific investigation into blood and the circulatory system. Still, 300 years would pass before Karl Landsteiner developed and proved his theory of four distinctive human blood types. Drew read of the hit-or-miss scientific processes that took place during those three centuries. Most of the crude attempts at blood transfusion during that time were disastrous, with a majority of the patients dying. Doctors tried many different techniques. Some doctors tried using many different types of animal blood. Others tried working with blood from dead human bodies. None of their varied attempts, however, proved to be successful.

By the time World War I started, methods had hardly improved. Doctors' inability to transfuse blood cost thousands upon thousands of lives. Drew read of an elementary blood bank, not much more than blood kept cool with a block of ice, used by the American Expeditionary Forces in France. Blood was given to those wounded in the trenches. This established without a doubt that patients suffering from shock and hemorrhage benefited greatly from the transfusion of blood. The way patients were given the blood, however, was inefficient and unreliable.

Scudder, too, had done extensive research on treatments for shock. It was quite clear to Scudder, Drew, and the entire medical community that a loss of blood led to shock. Shock was often fatal. Scudder's research stemmed from his travels to India, where he worked to battle cholera. There he learned that one could transfuse saltwater followed by whole blood with some success.

Yet when Scudder and Drew put their heads together along with the rest of the research team, they became stuck on the problem of preservation. How could red blood cells be kept from breaking down, a process called hemolysis, and releasing unacceptable levels of potassium into the blood?

Drew decided that there must be something in the blood itself that kept it from being successfully stored. He broke down the blood into its components and studied each one. He examined white blood cells. He discovered nothing new with regard to performing transfusions. The white blood cells would continue to fight infections and bacteria. The platelets would do what they do in transfusion, too—help blood to clot. He then examined the properties of the red blood cells. He concluded

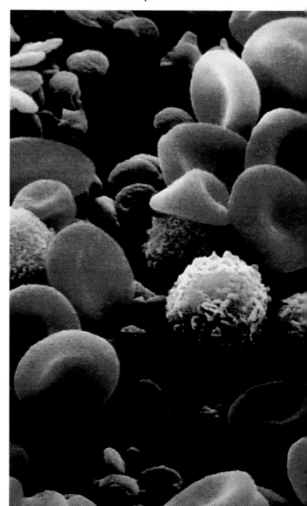

A photograph taken with an electron microscope of the parts of blood shows red blood cells, white blood cells, and platelets.

that they were the very essence of blood. But these cells were causing most of the transfusion and storage problems. They often broke down after being stored for a short period. And if it was incompatible with the patient's blood, the donated blood could cause serious illness, even death.

Drew and Scudder gathered all this data and used it to further their research. At the same time, Drew was performing surgery three days a week. As the research progressed, however, Scudder wanted Drew to decrease his surgery load and to concentrate more on scientific research. He went to Whipple and asked for more of Drew's time. Whipple said that he would give his consent if Drew agreed.

Scudder then went to Drew and argued his case. He pointed out that, by 1938, Europe was closer to another war every day. Once war broke out, blood would be essential.

Drew agreed. He now performed countless experiments with pathologists, biologists, chemists, and technicians. They went step-by-step through every possible method by which they might store blood.

Drew brought his discoveries back to Scudder. Telling him the obvious advantages of stored blood, Drew noted that the disadvantages of aged blood made it potentially dangerous. They did not know if blood that was kept in a preservative, such as sodium citrate, would become toxic over time. And if so, they did not know the property in blood that made it dangerous.

Scudder decided that they needed to have some answers by the following month—that was when a meeting was scheduled to begin exploring the idea of a blood bank.

Drew studied tirelessly. During the summer of 1938, he would work sometimes up to 18 hours a day. In September of that year, Neville Chamberlain, the prime minister of

England, returned from Germany delighted that he had reached a pact with Germany's Adolf Hitler. The pact, Chamberlain insisted, ensured "peace in our time." But it did just the opposite. Hitler understood that France and England would do nearly anything to avoid war. The world moved toward World War II.

Under the weight of this impending violence across the Atlantic Ocean, Drew continued to plug away at the research and experiments in 1938 and 1939. The more discoveries Drew and Scudder made, the more likely they might be to obtain funding for a blood bank. One conclusion all agreed on was that the longer the blood sat, the worse the effects of the transfusion. Sometimes the effect was a fever; other times, a chill. Sometimes a rash occurred, and in some cases there was jaundice, which is caused by liver malfunction.

A Week's Vacation, a Lifelong Love

It sometimes seemed to Drew as if he was working in a dark room where the rest of the world no longer existed. This, of course, was not true. Word got to Washington, D.C., about how well he was doing in the laboratory. Scudder continually reported to the Rockefeller Foundation, and the Foundation gave feedback to Dean Adams at Howard.

In the early spring of 1939, Drew received tangible evidence that he was not lost in a laboratory. Adams wrote a letter to Drew, asking him to accompany some of the Howard University staff to conferences at the John T. Andrews Memorial Clinic, part of the Tuskegee Institute, a black institution, in Tuskegee, Alabama. Adams invited Drew to give a talk on blood transfusions.

Drew was very busy, but he felt that it would be nice to talk with physicians who were treating patients. It would be even nicer to trade ideas with African-American doctors who were probably thirsty for the latest news from the scientific frontier.

Scudder agreed that Drew ought to take the trip; it was not the first time that he had attempted to get Drew to take some time off. Drew was convinced. He got on a train on April 2 and first went home to see his family. Then, with a group of doctors from Howard also headed to the conference, he continued down the East Coast by car to Alabama. The medical crew stopped for a dinner party in Atlanta, Georgia, at the house of a friend from Amherst, Mercer Cook, now a professor at Atlanta University.

At the party, Drew met Minnie Lenore Robbins (called "Lenore"), a lovely 28-year-old woman from Philadelphia, Pennsylvania. She was a teacher of home economics at Spelman College, the first school for black women in the United States. He was smitten with her, as she was with him. "The moment I met Charlie I knew he was a man to be reckoned with—and the man for me," she said later.

As was true in most other aspects of his life, Charles Drew was remarkably decisive in his love life. He went on to Tuskegee and participated in the clinic. Still, he could not stop thinking about Lenore Robbins. After the longest three days of his life, Drew dashed back to Atlanta and knocked on Cook's door. Cook gave him Lenore's address at Spelman.

She lived in the Bessie Strong dormitory on the Spelman College campus. Drew arrived there late at night. He rang the bell until the night matron answered. When he asked to see Miss Robbins, the matron politely refused. Drew would not take no for an answer. He swore he would go directly to

Robbins's room if the matron did not call her down to the gate. The matron gave in.

When Robbins arrived downstairs, she was stunned to see Drew standing there, with a look of love in his eyes. She was even more amazed when Drew proposed marriage. She found it incredible that a man would ask a woman to marry him after meeting her just three days earlier. But Charles Richard Drew was not an average man. When he knew that something was worthwhile, he pursued it to the fullest. When he met Lenore Robbins, he knew he must marry her. Sitting at the gate at the Bessie Strong dorm, Drew would not allow Lenore to reject his proposal.

In all good sense, she should have. But something about this serious young man captivated her. She was unable to say "no." Instead, she went with Drew to Mercer Cook's house, so Drew might continue to plead his case. Finally, she said "maybe."

Once back in New York, Drew almost flooded Robbins with ardent love letters and continuing pleas that she marry him: "I have moved through the days as one in a dream, lost in reverie, awed by the speed with which the moving finger of fate has pointed out the way I should go."

After months of letter writing and long-distance courtship, Minnie Lenore Robbins finally said "yes." The two were married on September 23, 1939, in Philadelphia, her hometown.

The newlyweds had neither the time nor the money for a honeymoon. They returned to New York City and lived in an apartment not far from Columbia Presbyterian. As Drew went to work each day, Lenore cleaned their small apartment, bought and prepared food for supper, and waited for her husband to return. She grew bored. She had lived

After months of courting her long distance, Drew married Minnie
Lenore Robbins in 1939. Here, the couple shares an evening out.

an active and challenging life filled with people and problems and solutions. Now she did nearly nothing, while her
husband performed surgery, did research, and labored on
his dissertation. She spent most of her time by herself.

When she told Charles that she wanted to go back to
teaching, he agreed that she ought to do more. But he
thought they might do something together. As a result of
the work that he and Scudder had put into the effort,
Columbia Presbyterian Hospital had started a blood bank
in August 1939. Drew was named medical director of the

program. The blood bank was now permanent at the hospital. The two came upon the idea that she might join him at the research lab. She could work as an assistant and help him keep records. She was smart, educated, and, as a former college teacher, familiar with the demands of the academic work her husband performed every day. Soon, with Scudder's approval, Lenore joined the research team at the Columbia Presbyterian laboratories.

It was fortunate that she did. She was familiar enough with his work that they could discuss at home problems to which Drew could not find solutions in the laboratory. One evening as Drew explained some of the fundamentals of blood and its components to her, he came up with an idea.

Plasma, which makes up more than half of the physical contents of blood, is a fluid that contains water, antibodies, hormones, nutrients, and proteins. More important, Drew reasoned, plasma does not contain red blood cells. The red blood cells are the troublemakers when it comes to blood-typing and transfusions. They are the cells that break down and cause hemolysis and jaundice. In addition, plasma contains a protein called fibrinogen that works as a clotting agent. Plasma might just be the answer the Columbia Presbyterian research team was looking for.

Drew threw himself into this new possibility. As he had done before, he researched the use of plasma in medical history. Drew and Scudder were not alone in contributing to the development of successful blood transfusions. Edwin J. Cohn, a professor of biological chemistry at Harvard University, discovered many important things about plasma. And others added what they had discovered to the body of knowledge about blood and plasma. Within a short period of time, Drew was convinced that using plasma made

THE PLASMA SOLUTION

The discovery of using plasma instead of whole blood in transfusions established a successful way to treat patients suffering from shock or severe burns.

The use of plasma was logical. Every time Drew and his team of scientists ran into problems with the storage of blood, the red blood cells were the culprits. Why not, then, separate the red blood cells from the plasma and see whether plasma alone would work? Plasma constitutes 55 percent of blood and has all the important elements needed for transfusion: water, nutrients, proteins, antibodies, and hormones. Most important, it has fibrinogen, a protein instrumental in the clotting of blood. Plasma transfusions allow the human body to achieve a fluid balance without doctors' having to worry about hemolysis, the breakdown of red blood cells, as plasma contains no red blood cells.

Plasma is much easier to store and save than whole blood. Also, plasma can be dried and then stored for many, many months. Dried plasma is reconstituted with sterile distilled water.

a great deal of sense in specific instances. However, being personally convinced of something and proving it scientifically are two different things.

But there was a war on—World War II. Not long after Drew felt comfortable with the progress of the plasma research, he and Scudder went to the Blood Transfusion Betterment Association conference. It was then that Drew's reputation as a world-renowned scientist and surgeon began to blossom. At the conference, he explained that he thought plasma would work in transfusions because it stored well. He said it could last nearly a month without refrigeration.

Drew's tireless research in New York led to the discovery
that plasma might be the key to storing blood successfully.

Dried, it could last even longer. More crucial, plasma transfusions worked best for people suffering from severe burns and shock from acute blood loss. That was precisely what happened to people most often in wartime. Plasma transfusions made sense.

Simultaneously, Drew worked on the last part of his dissertation, *Banked Blood*. When it was completed, Scudder declared it a masterpiece. Drew then took his oral exam for his doctorate. Again he performed flawlessly. Whipple considered Drew's intense research with Scudder in fluid and salt balance studies and work in organizing the blood bank at the Columbia Presbyterian Hospital outstanding. In June 1940, Columbia awarded Drew the degree of Doctor of Science in Medicine. Charles Drew became the first African American ever to achieve this honor.

Drew reasoned that what he had set out to do in New York was finished. "I guess I'll have to go to work now," he joked. He and Lenore headed to Washington, D.C. He seriously believed that what lay ahead was to be his most important work—he wished to advance the cause of African-American doctors.

Drew became an assistant professor of surgery at Howard University and a surgeon at Freedmen's Hospital. He was back home, but not for long.

CHAPTER FIVE

SERVICE TO A NATION; SERVICE TO A PEOPLE

The Drew family had grown just before its arrival in Washington, D.C. Roberta "Bebe" Drew, Charles and Lenore's first child, was born. And more changes were afoot. After only a one-month stay in Washington, in the fall of 1940, a telegram was sent directly to Howard University, requesting that Drew be allowed another leave of absence. The Blood Transfusion Betterment Association had created the position of medical supervisor for him. He was to be the liaison between the hospitals supplying plasma to Britain and the organizing board. Drew returned to New York City to direct America's Blood for Britain program.

Although the university granted Drew's leave, Lenore had difficulty with it. Since they had a new baby at home, Lenore could not move back to New York City. She would be alone in Washington. Drew knew, however, that Lenore could see the world beyond their living room. She told him that she would be the last person in the world who would want him to turn down such an exciting opportunity and such important work.

When Drew reached New York, John Bush, president of the Blood Transfusion Betterment Association, and Scudder were waiting for him. They went directly to Columbia Presbyterian. There they discussed how they might begin to gather blood to prepare the plasma they would ship to England. Bush expressed his concern that the main problem was bacterial contamination of plasma. Another concern was the lack of a uniform procedure for collecting blood and processing the plasma. For their part, Drew and Scudder wondered how they were going to get people to donate blood for strangers who were an ocean away.

The answer was a telephone number, SA 2-8590. Announcements had gone out over the radio waves of New York City telling people to call that number if they wanted to donate blood. Nine operators waited for a response. Within seconds the operators were swamped. Drew and Scudder watched as the switchboard lights blinked constantly. They were excited because suddenly they had all the blood they needed. What they needed even more now was a way of organizing the collection. That is where Drew's expertise played a crucial role.

He directed the donation effort and created a uniform procedure for collection. He made sure that those people drawing the blood were trained technicians. More important, he made sure that the process by which the laboratories separated the plasma from the rest of the blood was done in a very careful and clean manner. Of utmost importance to the success of the Blood for Britain project was keeping the separated plasma uncontaminated by bacteria, organisms that can cause illness.

Drew oversaw the procedure to ensure that well-trained people maintained carefully the sterility of the plasma. At the same time, he also standardized the entire process by which whole blood was collected for every single hospital in the country.

The Blood for Britain program proved to be a success. Thousands of lives were saved because of the plasma they received from transfusions. In time, Britain was able to collect enough blood from the British to establish its own banks, and, in January 1941, America's Blood for Britain program ended. Drew was then given a new job: analyzing the program in case the United States should enter World War II. The Blood Transfusion Betterment Association relied on his genius every chance they could, praising Drew's organizational as well as medical expertise.

One would have thought that Drew's work in New York was done and that he could now return to his wife and baby and his job in Washington, D.C. But it did not work out that way. Drew was asked by DeWitt Smith, of the American Red Cross, to be the medical director of its nationwide collection of blood for the U.S. Armed Forces. Drew wanted desperately to get back to his family. He was lonely, and he missed them. He also still had very important work to do back at Howard, training African-American doctors. Still, the nation was about to go to war. Lenore, the baby, and his students would have to wait.

By February 3, 1941, Drew had the American Red Cross blood-collection project up and running. Soon afterward, he and his team began using mobile units to collect blood. They sent buses with sophisticated blood-collection equipment out on the road to people who lived far from hospitals. This was a good idea, because many people would not go out of their way to donate blood. If a mobile unit was close by, however, people were willing to give. The mobile unit became a regular feature of the American Red Cross's blood drive. Even today, American Red Cross mobile units collect blood in different cities and towns.

Drew's work for the Red Cross went very well until the U.S. Armed Forces informed the Red Cross that only blood from white people would be accepted. The U.S. War Department realized that this made no sense but issued the following statement anyway:

For reasons not biologically convincing but which are commonly recognized psychologically important in America, it is not deemed advisable to collect and mix Caucasian and Negro blood indiscriminately for later administration to members of the military forces.

In effect, government leaders were saying that they knew this was wrong but that they would go along with it because many white Americans had expressed a desire to have only white blood in the program. Shortly after this notice had been issued, Drew learned that African Americans in the South were not allowed to donate blood at all. How strange, Drew thought, that while the U.S. Army rejected "black" blood, the man who ran the program to collect blood for the same army had "black" blood coursing through his veins.

Drew (far left) stands with members of Columbia Presbyterian's mobile blood collection unit. For the first time, people could donate blood without having to travel far from home.

During World War II the American Red Cross
provided medical supplies to war-torn regions.

But the U.S. Armed Forces at that time were known for
their unfair policies regarding blacks. Whites and blacks
served in separate units in all branches of the service, with
the exception of the Marine Corps. (Integration of the military did not begin until 1945, and even then it was on an
experimental basis. Full integration occurred in 1950, at the
beginning of the Korean War.)

Charles Drew

The Armed Forces were not alone in making racist policies and statements. Congressman John E. Rankin of Mississippi stood on the floor of the U.S. Congress and spoke these words of hatred and bigotry:

Let doctors throughout the country see that no one can tell the consequences of pumping the blood of Negro races into the veins of those children. The chances are that it should crop out in the child of the one so treated. This is one of the most dangerous and dastardly proposals that has ever been ventured by these enemies of our form of government and our way of life.

Drew could not bear to listen to this ridiculousness any longer. He had to speak out. In a public statement, he said:

I feel that the recent ruling of the United States Army and Navy regarding the refusal of colored blood donors is an indefensible one from any point of view. As you know, there is no scientific basis for the separation of the bloods of different races except on the basis of the individual blood types or groups.

In the face of this controversy, then-secretary of war Henry Stimson reasserted that the U.S. Armed Forces would remain segregated. Black troops would continue to take their orders from white officers. Blacks would not be promoted to higher ranks. He concluded with a statement that Charles Richard Drew's entire life proved was a lie: "Leadership is not imbedded in the Negro race."

In April of that same year, Drew resigned as assistant director and medical director of the national blood program. Some speculated that he resigned because he was angry

Even though they remained segregated in
World War II, African-American soldiers
fought heroically for their country.

Charles Drew

with the racist policies of the U.S. Armed Forces in particular and the U.S. government in general.

Others guessed that he came to realize that he would never be named director because he was an African American, and so left. However, Burke Syphax, a friend of Drew's from Freedmen's Hospital, may have had the correct answer: "Charlie was disturbed about the rumors, of course. But his returning to Howard was another thing entirely. There had always been sort of an unspoken agreement that he'd someday return as chief of surgery. He always planned on coming back home."

DREW THE EDUCATOR

In some ways, Drew's involvement in the racial controversies generated by the U.S. Armed Forces cemented his belief that he ought to devote himself to the education of African-American doctors. He felt that he could best help other African Americans by returning to his positions at Howard University and Freedmen's Hospital. To add weight and significance to his teaching, he wanted to enhance his standing by being certified as a surgeon by the American Board of Surgery.

He did just that by traveling to Baltimore, Maryland, where he had coached at Morgan College. There he submitted to examination by a panel of experts from Johns Hopkins Medical School, one of the most respected medical schools in the country. The expert panel questioned Drew about his specialty, which was fluid balance in the body. They found his answers to be so interesting and knowledgeable that they asked other examiners to hear what he had to say.

Students at Howard University and Freedmen's Hospital looked to Drew for inspiration. Here, he addresses a class of nursing school graduates.

Needless to say, he passed the examination rather easily. So easily, in fact, that Drew was invited to be an examiner for the American Board of Surgery the following year.

His next stop was farther down the Atlantic coast to his home in Washington, D.C. After his joyful reunion with Lenore and Bebe, Charles returned to Howard University and Freedmen's Hospital.

Things were different in April 1941. Dean Numa Adams had died. Edward Howes had returned to Yale. Now Joseph L. Johnson was acting dean. He welcomed Drew back to his position as assistant professor of surgery.

Soon afterward, Drew was certified as a diplomate of the American Board of Surgery, another first for an African-American doctor. This qualification as a medical specialist acknowledged his advanced training. The administration of Howard University realized that he should no longer hold the title of assistant professor. In the summer of 1941, he was appointed professor of surgery at Howard and chief surgeon at Freedmen's Hospital. Once again, Charles Drew had more than enough work to do.

When Drew gave a lecture, students not even enrolled in his class crowded the classroom. The students considered him the best teacher in the medical school. And when he made the rounds of the wards at Freedmen's, every resident and intern who could make it followed him closely and listened to every word he spoke. They did so not only because he was brilliant and a good speaker but because they believed in his mission.

That mission was to create an institution that could raise African-American doctors to the standards white doctors enjoyed. As he said, "We must stimulate desire in those we teach. A desire not simply to be good surgeons, but to spread themselves around, pass it on, as it were. They must get into the mainstream of surgery and come up to the level of the whites." Drew practiced what he preached. He was not just a good surgeon, but one who spread himself around. Some think he spread himself around too much. Surely his family sometimes did. Although he lived only two blocks away from his office on the Howard campus, he was rarely home.

This is not to say that he neglected his family. Later in 1941, the Drews rejoiced over the birth of their second child, Charlene. Over the next few years, two more children, Rhea and Charles, Jr., would join the family. Lenore explained that Drew was a good parent who gave his all when he was with his family. As his wife already understood, and as his children would learn to understand, Drew's purpose in

Drew loved his family (from left to right), Roberta, Charlene, Rhea, Lenore, and Charles, Jr., and enjoyed spending time with them.

life was very grand in scope. He was not meant to be just a great doctor and teacher. He was meant to be a living inspiration for other African-American doctors.

Drew was aware of this task. He may have understood his special position in history as a result of receiving constant recognition for excellence. In 1942, Drew was awarded the E. S. Jones Award for Research in Medical Science. The following year he was invited to join the American-Soviet Committee on Science.

In 1944, he became chief of staff of Freedmen's Hospital, after which he scurried all over Washington. He lobbied and pleaded with representatives and senators for additional funding for Freedmen's. His argument made a lot of sense. He told various congressmen from the South how much money their states were saving by having their African-American doctors trained at Howard and Freedmen's.

They agreed. His hard work resulted in the hospital's budget being increased from $1 million to $3.5 million. He was only 40 years old, but he had already reached the pinnacle of medical teaching and medical administration. Most people labor their entire lives and never get even near the top. Drew did it in half a lifetime.

Still, he was not through. That same year, in 1944, he earned the Spingarn Medal, given by the National Association for the Advancement of Colored People (NAACP) for the "highest or noblest achievement by an American Negro." The award read:

To Dr. Charles Drew for his outstanding work in blood plasma. Dr. Drew's research in this field led to the establishment of a blood plasma bank which served as one of the models for the widespread system of blood banks used by the

American Red Cross. Dr. Drew was appointed full-time Medical Director for the blood plasma project in Great Britain. The report on this work was published and served as a guide for later developments for the United States Army and for the armies of our Allies.

Only two other men of science had won this award: Ernest Everett Just, in 1915, and George Washington Carver, in 1923. Just was a renowned zoologist. George Washington Carver was a famous scientist and agriculturalist who invented peanut butter and other important peanut products. Drew was shocked to receive the prestigious award, as he had not worked in plasma research for three years. Drew pointed out that his focus now was in the field of surgery and that his work in blood banking was done. It was something that the world would soon recognize. Many people wondered if the award had been given to him in part to make the racist exclusion of African Americans from donating blood look that much more foolish.

It became clear that others understood Drew was a surgeon first and foremost when later that year, he was named chairman of the Surgical Section of the National Medical Society. His place in the annals of surgery grew even more secure when he became a fellow of the International College of Surgeons in 1946. And in 1949, in the closest thing that Charles Drew had ever had to a vacation, he had the honor of touring Europe as one of four surgical consultants to the surgeon general of the U.S. Army.

But to Drew himself, his biggest achievement was the way in which his students performed. In 1948, some of his residents took their exams for certification by the American Board of Surgery. They took the same test he had taken.

Drew was nervous. If his students did not pass the test, other hospitals would find reasons not to take these black surgeons for specialist training. But the great teacher and motivator need not have worried. Two of the residents scored higher than anyone else who took the exam, which was given to students from the very best medical schools in the country. Suddenly, the medical world had no choice but to acknowledge the intelligence, drive, and training of these African-American doctors from Howard University Medical School.

A Crusade Written and Lived

Drew's goal of educating others did not stop with medical students. He wrote articles for publication and often spoke publicly about the difficulties that blacks faced in the sciences. One of his underlying messages was that to erase the ugly bias that many white Americans held against blacks, African Americans must become high achievers.

Perhaps Drew's greatest source of irritation was the refusal of some chapters of the American Medical Association (AMA) to admit African Americans. A doctor who was not a member of the association was not able to go to meetings and learn of the latest techniques and discoveries. And even though the policy of the AMA was to accept blacks, the organization did nothing to stop the discrimination. The result was that black doctors in the South were not members of the AMA.

This seemed utterly ridiculous to Drew. He often published his scientific studies in the *Journal of the American Medical Association* (*JAMA*). So did other African-American

Drew, seen here two days before his death, often spoke of the injustices faced by African Americans who sought degrees in medicine.

physicians and scientists. W. Montague Cobb, Drew's long-time friend and colleague at Howard, put together a list of articles that were written by blacks and published in *JAMA*. It numbered more than 2,200. Drew himself had written 21 of them. Still, the AMA did nothing to keep the local chapters from excluding black doctors. In response,

Drew wrote a very angry letter to Morris Fishbein, the editor of the journal:

> *One hundred years of racial bigotry and fatuous pretense; one hundred years of gross disinterest in a large section of the American people whose medical voice it purports to be—as regards the problem of Negroes which it raised in 1870; one hundred years with no progress to report. A sorry record.*

In spite of his harsh language, Drew lost this fight. The local chapters of the AMA of the South continued to exclude blacks, and the national AMA continued to do nothing about it. But Drew continued to write to Fishbein in order to voice his anger. The AMA did not correct the problem until 1968, long after Drew's death.

This was not the only time Drew used his writing skills to point out the problems faced by African Americans. One paper in particular, his essay "Negro Scholars in Scientific Research," stands out. The basic point he made in the article was his concern about the state of blacks in America in general and in the field of science in particular. By writing this piece and delivering it at the annual meeting of the Association for the Study of Negro Life and History, in New York City, on October 30, 1949, he tried to show how far African Americans had come as scientists and where it was they needed to advance. He wrote:

> *[T]he Negro in the field of physical sciences has not only opened a small passageway to the outside world, but is carving a road in many untrod areas, along which later generations will find it more easy to travel. The breaching out these walls and laying of this road has not been, and is not easy.*

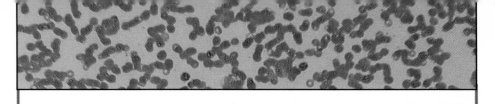

THE DREW CHILDREN

When Charles Drew died in 1950, he left a record of care for his community. He worked hard to help people with his blood-transfusion research. He excelled at teaching others to be good doctors. He also was dedicated to his family. Probably the part of his legacy that Drew would be proudest of is how productive his and Lenore's children are.

Their oldest child, Roberta (called "Bebe" after the initials of "blood bank"), grew to be a homemaker and mother in Columbia, Maryland.

Charles and Lenore's son, Charles, Jr., followed in his father's footsteps in a very important way: He became a teacher. He understood the value of teaching others, a lesson that his parents would be very pleased to know their son had learned.

Their youngest daughter, Rhea, is a lawyer who, like her father, has devoted much of her efforts to helping the African-American community. At one time she worked for the NAACP's Legal Defense Fund.

Their middle daughter, Charlene Drew Jarvis, was a neurobiologist at the National Institutes of Health. Although she then ran for mayor of Washington, D.C., she did not win. She is now, however, councilwoman of Ward 4 in Washington, D.C. Charlene has not only followed in her father's footsteps but has taken to heart his sense of debt to the community.

All of the children are a tribute to their mother's devotion and their father's example.

Drew never lost sight of his responsibility as both a parent and a teacher. He also never lost sight of his responsibility as a role model for young African Americans interested in science and medicine. He took all of these roles very seriously. That is why he spent the time and effort being a great teacher at Howard University Medical School.

It is also why he wrote many articles and gave speeches in New York City and elsewhere.

Because he was Freedmen's chief surgeon, Drew had many duties. One was to represent the hospital at the medical conference and free clinic at the John A. Andrew Memorial Hospital in Tuskegee, Alabama. Drew had been attending this conference for ten years. In April 1950, he chose to drive instead of fly to be with three other men who were going to the conference, Walter Johnson, John Ford, and Samuel Bullock. They agreed to take turns driving.

Drew took his turn early the next morning, April 1, just outside of Richmond, Virginia. He rested once and then started up again. But the rest was not enough. He had been in surgery the entire day and night the day before. Drew could not keep his eyes open. "All I remember is suddenly coming awake and noticing that the sky wasn't exactly where it ought to be," Bullock recalled.

Bullock had shouted, "Hey, Charlie!" but it was too late. Drew failed to straighten out the car. It went off the road and into a field, turning over three times. Johnson was uninjured. He helped Bullock, who only had a cut on his hand, out of the car. Ford had been thrown from the car and had a broken arm.

Drew, though, had gotten his right foot caught under the brake pedal. Otherwise, he would have been thrown from the car. Instead, the car rolled over on top of him. When the three others reached him, he was severely injured. His left leg was almost completely severed, and he was in shock. An ambulance arrived and took Drew to the Alamance General Hospital, in Burlington, North Carolina. There, two brothers, Drs. Harold and Charles Kernodle, attended to him. They tried to resuscitate him. They gave him oxygen and administered glucose intravenously. "But he was critically injured, in a state in which there was very little that we could do for him," said Charles Kernodle more than 40 years after the accident. He added that they had not given him blood because it would take at least an hour to match his blood type. By then it was too late.

Dr. Charles Richard Drew died less than an hour after arriving at the hospital. He was just 45 years old. He left behind a legacy almost too great to fit into one life, let alone a life cut short.

THE

LEGACY

oward University held a wake for Dr. Charles Richard Drew in the university chapel. The funeral was on April 5, 1950, at the Nineteenth Street Baptist Church. At the service were Allen Whipple, John Scudder, and many of Drew's patients. The president of Howard, Mordecai Johnson, spoke of Drew's life as "a life which crowds into a handful of years significance so great men will never be able to forget it."

The *Washington Post* ran an editorial about Drew that was entered into the Congressional Record by Hubert Humphrey: "He will be missed not alone by his race but by his whole profession and by men everywhere who value scientific devotion and integrity."

Worldwide, millions of people owe their lives to
Charles Drew and the blood plasma research he
did that led to the establishment of blood banks.

The American Red Cross

The American Red Cross, the organization of which Drew was the medical director in the early 1940s, has come a long way in the past 50 years. It now has a two-part mission.

The first part is its disaster-relief work. The Red Cross does two things in the case of disasters. It prepares communities for impending disasters, such as hurricanes or tornadoes. And it responds to a situation after a disaster has occurred. The Red Cross provides temporary shelter for victims, including cots to sleep on. Sometimes food is provided as well.

In 1995, a human-made disaster occurred in Oklahoma City when the federal building was bombed. The American Red Cross provided rescue help and as much emergency medical assistance as they could. One of the major services the organization provided to those in Oklahoma City was mental-health counseling for people who were shocked and traumatized by the bombing.

The second part of the American Red Cross's mission is to supply half of the nation's blood needs. Six million units (a unit is a single donation) of blood are collected every year. The organization has nearly perfected its methods for the collection of blood. The rate of infections from blood transfusions is now hundreds and hundreds of times lower than it has ever been.

The American Red Cross collects half of the amount of blood that the United States needs for its blood supply. The rest is collected by other organizations. However, shortages may occur and there are many reasons for this. First among these is the fear that by giving blood, one can contract the human immunodeficiency virus (HIV) the virus that causes acquired immunodeficiency syndrome (AIDS). This is untrue. There has not been a single case of someone contracting any disease by giving blood. Another reason is that people have less time to volunteer their help to the Red Cross and less time to give blood. In the 1990s, there has been a 2 percent decline in blood donations every year—a fact that would no doubt sadden

Dr. Charles Drew. Even with these difficulties, the American Red Cross continues to do an incredible job of caring for the needs of Americans.

The American Red Cross Disaster Services provided food to this young victim of Hurricane Andrew in 1992.

Schools and hospitals have been named after Charles Drew. His portrait hangs in the National Portrait Gallery; in the American Red Cross national headquarters in Washington, D.C.; and at the National Institutes of Health in Bethesda, Maryland. In 1976, the award to honor a person who advances the medical education of African Americans and other minorities was named the Charles R. Drew Commemorative Medal. In 1981, the U.S. Postal Service issued a stamp with Dr. Drew's picture on it to commemorate his scientific work. In 1994, the American Red Cross honored Drew by naming a training facility after him. The Charles Drew Biomedical Institute serves to educate and train staff in the latest blood-collecting techniques and to ensure the safety of the nation's blood supply.

Charles Drew left a remarkable legacy—a legacy of actually three parts. One, the world will always remember Drew's scientific research on blood banking and the medical advances that have come from his work in the laboratories. Two, the African-American community in the United States is a safer and healthier place because of Drew's teaching of black doctors at Howard University Medical School and Freedmen's Hospital.

The third part of Drew's legacy, however, is not positive. After his death, a rumor started to circulate in the African-American community. Many people believed that the doctor had not received adequate medical attention at Alamance General Hospital because he was black. Some believed that Drew was not given a blood transfusion because the blood in the hospital was "white" blood, which black patients were not allowed to receive.

How this rumor started is difficult to know. But many people knew how strange it was for a black man to be the medical director of the American Red Cross blood drive at the same time that blacks in the South were turned away from blood-collection centers. Some may have thought that this same black man of science, when in desperate need of blood from a hospital in the South, would be denied. In truth, however, that is not the case.

Nonetheless, as late as 1982, more than 30 years after the automobile accident that killed him, newspapers were reporting as "fact" that Dr. Drew had been denied blood at the hospital because he was black. Finally, Drew's daughter Charlene Drew Jarvis, at that time a candidate for mayor of Washington, D.C., decided that she needed to find out the truth about the incidents surrounding her father's death. Charlene Drew Jarvis wrote letters to everyone she could think of who was connected to the accident and waited for replies. She got her answers.

Samuel Bullock, one of the doctors who was in the car that early morning with Drew at the time of the tragic accident, remembers that although Alamance General Hospital was not one of the best hospitals in the country, Drew had received the best care available. "Racism was alive and well then," Bullock said, "but on that occasion, it was not the case.... Charles Drew simply was not discriminated against. I was in that emergency room."

Charles Mason Quick, an African-American general practitioner who was a 35-year-old doctor at the time of the accident, calls the rumor a "perpetual lie." "I'm a black man," Quick said, "and this is my state. I know you can indict North Carolina for a number of things. But you can't indict her for this."

In the end, Charlene Drew Jarvis decided that the evidence she gathered was overwhelming. The rumor that had circulated for many years was false. Her father did not die from racist medical treatment. Charles Drew died from the injuries he suffered in that tragic car crash.

Scientific Legacy

The medical advances that came from Drew's lifelong hard work are still with us today. It is not an exaggeration to say that thousands of people owe their lives to his genius. If not for his work on the use of plasma as a blood substitute, patients throughout the world would have died from blood transfusions. In some ways, though, this is just the surface of his impact on science and medicine.

His research efforts benefited Karl Landsteiner (the Nobel Prize winner who had discovered blood types), whom Drew sent blood supplies that he could not use. Landsteiner used the blood in his work that led to the discovery of the rhesus (Rh) factor. The Rh factor is a protein found in blood that can induce hemolytic reactions. Landsteiner's discovery enabled babies with Rh disease to be delivered safely, when before they had not. In fact, the entire field of obstetrics, the medical science of birth, has benefited both directly and indirectly from Drew's research on blood.

Moreover, every scientist who has specialized in the transfusion of blood and plasma has used Charles Drew's studies as background. They have looked at the work done by Drew and Scudder and analyzed the data to create new ways of dealing with injured patients. Techniques for handling problems of blood sterilization and contamination are far more advanced. As a result, blood transfusions are much more sophisticated, and more successful. Medical

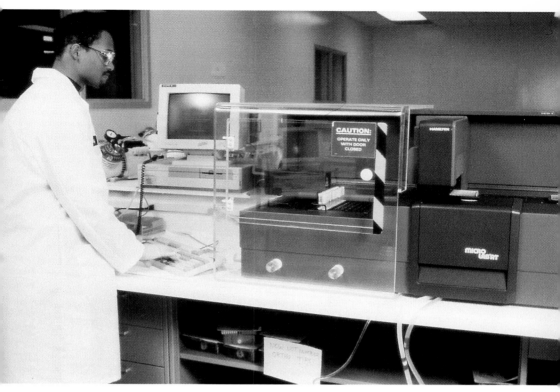

A Red Cross technologist tests for antibodies to
hepatitis C. Thanks to methods established by Drew,
the blood supply is safer today than in the past.

technology has come up with a way to store frozen blood
for ten years, with only a small portion of the red blood cells
breaking down. Although some synthetic blood substitutes
like PVP—polyvinylpyrrolidone—were first introduced in
Germany, other blood substitutes are in use in the United
States today. A patient today is unlikely to have the problems that Drew's patients did in the 1940s, because of
scientific advances based on Drew's work at Columbia
Presbyterian Hospital. Nonetheless, problems still exist in
the field of blood transfusions.

Blood banks are now common throughout the world. Drew implemented standard procedures for the collection and storage of blood. Now almost every hospital uses the cleaner and safer methods of blood collecting and storage he devised for the American Red Cross.

Drew did not come up with the idea that plasma was an ideal blood substitute simply because it did not contain any problematic red blood cells. He first examined all the components of plasma. This study led to some very important findings. More than just one type of protein is found in plasma. One of them is albumin. There is more albumin in plasma than any other protein. Albumin attracts water, and may be used as a blood substitute.

Gamma globulin is also found in plasma. It is taken from donated whole blood, processed, and used to treat patients exposed to a variety of diseases.

A photograph taken with an electron microscope shows a red blood cell with a yellow covering of fibrin—the protein made from fibrinogen when blood clots.

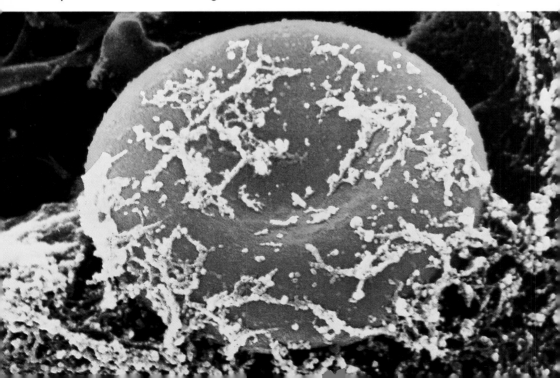

Blood Transfusions in the Age of AIDS

Today, there is great concern over the use of blood transfusions. People are afraid of contracting the human immunodeficiency virus (HIV), which causes AIDS (acquired immunodeficiency syndrome). In truth, the risk of contracting HIV today is less than it has ever been. Ten years ago, the documented risk of contracting HIV from a transfusion was 1 in 2,500 transfusions. Now the screening process is far more sophisticated. The risk now is extremely small—1 in 420,000 transfusions.

In fact, a greater risk in blood transfusions has always been the risk of contracting hepatitis. Hepatitis has not been in the newspapers and on television as much as AIDS has been, but it is very dangerous. In 1965, the risk of contracting hepatitis from a blood transfusion was about 1 in 10. That is a very frightening risk. By 1990, the risk had improved to 1 in 3,000. In 1992, an improved test enabled screening for hepatitis C, the most common form of the disease. Now the risk of contraction is 1 in 100,000.

Furthermore, blood-donation centers do a better job of screening donors than they have before. They ask potential donors lots of questions. When a potential donor fails the screening process, his or her name is entered into the memory banks of the computer. The person is registered as having incompatible blood.

Fibrinogen, another protein in plasma, helps blood to clot. When doctors perform surgery that lasts a long time, they may transfuse plasma containing fibrinogen into the patient to make sure that the patient does not bleed too much.

Perhaps the most important part of Drew's work as it relates to science today is the methods he used. He was an expert organizer. He helped the entire United States collect enough blood for the war effort. Now the United States, indeed the world, is faced with the AIDS epidemic. Because of Drew's efforts, others now know that it is possible to create methods by which all hospitals can deal with a single problem. Moreover, major national medical associations realize that Drew's focus on organization made lots of sense. Organization is as important a part of addressing a nation-wide medical problem as is the actual scientific discovery that corrects the problem.

Teaching Legacy

Some believe that Drew's greatest contribution to medicine was just what he thought it would be: his teaching at Howard University Medical School and Freedmen's Hospital. Charles D. Watts recollected, "Why, with a name like his after his work in blood, he could have named his future. He could have gone into practice.... There was no end to his alternatives. Instead, he came back to Howard as a teacher, and at great personal sacrifice."

Clearly, Drew believed that this sacrifice was one worth making. As he had told John Beattie when he was in medical school, the teaching of black doctors was as much a frontier as blood research was. He took teaching as seriously as he did blood research. LaSalle D. Leffall, later the head of surgical training at Howard, remembered how strict Drew was as a teacher: "[Y]ou knew he was angry about something. Really angry, I mean.... His eyes would flash. And he would flush beet-red. And you would know he had had it."

Drew lived by the ideal that standards of excellence were necessary. Samuel Bullock, a man who had known Drew from the time he was in high school at Dunbar in

Washington and who was one of the men with him in the car crash explained: "That man was a perfectionist from the first day I met him, and I'd known him since high school. He thrived on doing things—and having others do them—that he could take pride in."

When he joined the staff at Howard Medical School and Freedmen's Hospital, the facilities were substandard. Because these were two of the schools that produced the majority of African-American doctors, black doctors in the United States

Dr. Drew meets with a group of residents at Howard. Drew trained many young people to be excellent doctors and surgeons.

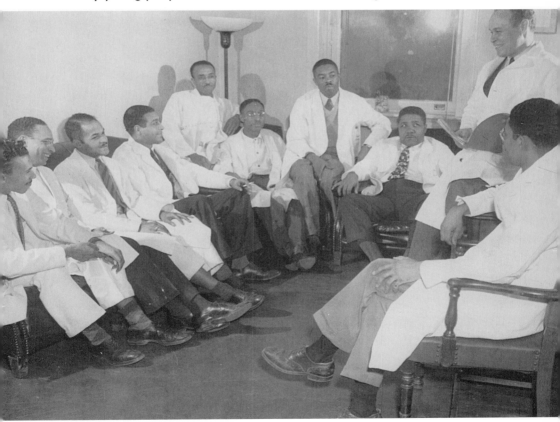

The Legacy

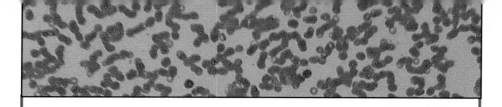

Drew's Proteges

As of 1980, eight of Charles Drew's former students were extremely prominent men in the world of medicine. Merle B. Herriford was an outstanding urologist at Homer Phillips Hospital in St. Louis, Missouri; Oswald W. Hoffler was the chief of surgery at the Norfolk Virginia Community Hospital; LaSalle D. Leffall was the chief of surgery at Howard University; C. Waldo Scott held the same position at Whittaker Hospital in Newport News, Virginia; Mitchell Spellman was the dean of the Charles Richard Drew Post-Graduate School, in Los Angeles, California; Charles D. Watts was the medical director of North Carolina Mutual Insurance Company; Jack White was the director of the Howard University Cancer Prevention Center; and Asa G. Yancy was the medical director of the Grady Teaching Hospital, in Atlanta, Georgia. This is just the tip of the Drew "teaching iceberg."

"He helped prepare a whole generation of surgeons, and a whole new thrust in training," explained Watts. "And what he did at Howard didn't collapse when he died. It was continued, very ably, by later chief surgeons: James R. Laurey, Clarence S. Greene, and LaSalle Leffall. Black surgical training has never been the same."

were getting inferior training. More important even, was the fact that black patients were getting inferior treatment. Charles Drew did everything in his power to correct this.

In the nine years between 1941 and 1950, Drew almost single-handedly prepared more than half of the black surgeons who passed the American Board of Surgery test for certification. Then he did something that many of the Howard Medical School faculty objected to. He encouraged the truly excellent surgeons he taught to go to other hospitals and medical schools to specialize in subspecialties.

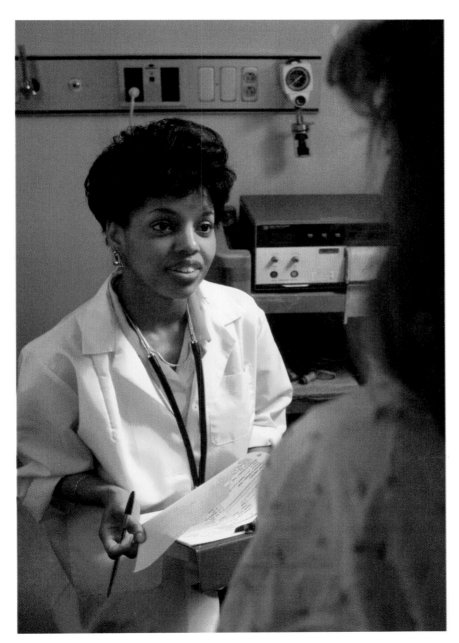

Drew encouraged a new generation of African-
American doctors to excel in their fields.

A lot of his students were the African-American pioneers in gynecology, neurosurgery, cardiovascular surgery, and other medical specialties. Some at Howard thought that this took the best students away from Howard. Watts thought it was a good idea, though: "Charlie was a believer in the vanguard. Many of these fields had only recently been developing. They were the focus of new research, of exciting new discoveries. Why shouldn't blacks be encouraged to try and enter them?"

Drew knew that his name was famous in the field of science, and he used that name to help Howard Medical School. Sometimes this annoyed people who might have been a little jealous. "If a group in New York wanted to do something for Howard, they didn't call the president— they telephoned Drew," said Watts. "That created a few problems."

Drew did not worry about what others thought about his methods, because he knew why he was doing it the way he was. The results of this concern and care were astounding. Based on Drew's example and efforts during his short teaching life, African-American enrollment in medical schools rose substantially from 350 in 1939 to 588 in 1948.

The enormity of Dr. Charles Richard Drew's impact on the African-American medical community went beyond anything anyone could have imagined. His impact on surgery and blood research was also huge. Drew led a life that was completely devoted to the betterment of humankind. Few other people have succeeded in this goal—whether in research, teaching, sports, or family—to the degree that Charles Drew did.

Glossary

AIDS Acquired immunodeficiency syndrome; the disease caused by HIV, or the human immunodeficiency virus. In AIDS, the human body's immune system is severely weakened, and consequently the body cannot fight other infections.

albumin A protein found in blood, egg whites, plants and animal tissues, and fluids. It can dissolve in water.

anemia A condition in which the blood is deficient in hemoglobin.

arteries Tubes that carry blood away from the heart.

blood bank A place where collected blood or plasma is stored for future use in blood transfusions.

blood types Also called blood groups; four main groups into which blood is separated. The four groups are A, B, AB, and O.

cadaver A dead body.

capillaries The smallest blood vessels found in the circulatory system. They connect the arteries and veins.

circulatory system The system of blood vessels and tissues that carry blood throughout the body.

discrimination The act of responding to or treating someone unfairly because of that person's beliefs such as religion, or physical characteristics, such as skin color or sex.

fibrin A protein made from fibrinogen when blood clots.

fibrinogen A protein found in plasma that is converted to fibrin when blood clots.

gamma globulin A protein found in plasma. It helps the body to fight against disease.

glucose A sugar that is the basic source of energy in the body.

Great Depression A period in history in which millions of people lost their jobs, homes, and savings because of an economic collapse that occurred in 1929.

hemoglobin A protein found in red blood cells. It helps to transport oxygen from the lungs to tissues in the body and it carries carbon dioxide away from the tissues to the lungs.

hemolysis A process in which healthy red blood cells break down, causing anemia and jaundice

hemorrhage A severe discharge of blood.

hepatitis A disease of the liver that is caused by a virus and is marked by inflammation. This disease can cause a person to experience jaundice, fever, and weakness.

HIV Human immunodeficiency virus; the virus that causes AIDS. HIV attacks and destroys healthy white blood cells called lymphocytes. As it does so, the virus multiplies in the body, causing the immune system to weaken. HIV is spread from person to person by body fluids and contaminated blood.

hormones Chemical substances produced by the body, which enter the bloodstream and have effect on organs.

jaundice A yellowing of the skin and the white part of the eyes.

lymphocyte A type of white blood cell that is important in protecting the body's immune system.

plasma One of the four main parts of blood; it is the liquid part of blood.

platelets One of the four main parts of blood; cell fragments in blood that help blood to clot.

proteins Naturally occurring substances that are found in all living cells.

red blood cells One of the four main parts of blood. These disk-shaped cells contain hemoglobin.

residency A period of advanced training in a specialty such as surgery for a physician.

segregation The act of separating one racial group, such as African Americans, from another. For a period in American history African Americans were forced to use separate schools and public facilities.

shock A dangerous condition in which the body is severely weakened due to a reduction in volume of circulating blood. It can occur after a serious injury.

sodium citrate A compound that is used to prevent blood from clotting.

transcript An official, written record of a student's grades received during high school or college.

transfusion The act of transferring blood from one individual to another.

veins Tubes that carry blood to the heart.

white blood cells One of the four main parts of blood. These cells help to fight off disease and infections.

Further Reading

Brodie, James Michael. *Created Equal: The Lives and Ideas of Black American Innovators*. New York: William Morrow, 1993.

Bryan, Jenny. *The Pulse of Life: The Circulatory System*. Morristown, NJ: Silver Burdett Press, 1993.

Hayden, Robert C. *Eleven African-American Doctors*. New York: Twenty-First Century Books, 1992.

Mahone-Lonesome, Robyn. *Charles Drew*. New York: Chelsea House, 1990.

McKissack, Patricia and Fredrick. *African-American Scientists: A Proud Heritage*. Brookfield, Connecticut: The Millbrook Press, 1994.

Parramon, Merce. *How Our Blood Circulates*. New York: Chelsea House, 1994.

Talmadge, Katherine S. *The Life of Charles Drew*. New York: Twenty-First Century Books, 1992.

Weatherford, Carole. *Remember Me: A Legacy of African-Americans*. New York: African American Family Press, 1994.

Wolfe, Rinna Evelyn. *Charles Richard Drew, M.D.* New York: Franklin Watts, 1991.

Sources

Afro-American Encyclopedia. Miami, FL: Educational Book Publishers, 1974.

Bims, Hamilton. "Charles Drew's 'Other' Medical Revolution," *Ebony*. February 1974, pp. 88–96.

Bittker, Anne S. "Charles Richard Drew, M.D.," *Negro History Bulletin*. November 1973, pp. 144–148.

Brodie, James Michael. *Created Equal: The Lives and Ideas of Black American Innovators*. New York: William Morrow and Company, 1993.

Cobb, W. Montague. "Charles Richard Drew, M.D., 1904–1950." *Journal of the National Medical Association*. July 1950, pp. 238–246.

"Dr. Charles R. Drew: Pioneer in Blood." *Encore*, April 4, 1977.

Drew, Charles. R. *Banked Blood: A Study in Blood Preservation*. Doctoral Thesis, Columbia University, June 1940.

———. "Negro Scholars in Scientific Research." *Journal of Negro History*. April 1950, pp. 135–149.

Drew, Lenore Robbins. "Unforgettable Charlie Drew," *Oracle*. Spring 1979, pp. 7–12, (Reprinted from *Reader's Digest*, March 1978).

Drew-Jarvis, Charlene. "Needed: Black Americans to Save Black American Lives." *The Washington Post*, February 13, 1994.

Dupuy, R. Ernest, and Trevor, N. *The Encyclopedia of Military History: From 3500 B.C. to the Present*, 2nd Ed. Rev. New York: Harper & Row, 1986.

Encyclopedia of American Biography. New York: Harper & Row, 1974.

Haber, Louis. *Black Pioneers of Science and Invention.*
New York: Harcourt, 1970.

Hardwick, Richard. *Charles Richard Drew: Pioneer in Blood Research.* New York: Scribner's Sons, 1967.

Hirsch, E. D., Jr., Kett, Joseph F., Trefil, James. *The Dictionary of Cultural Literacy: What Every American Needs to Know,* 2nd Ed. Rev. Boston: Houghton Mifflin Company, 1993.

Humphrey, Hubert D. "Dr. Charles R. Drew," *Congressional Record,* (10 Apr 50), 81st Cong., 2nd sess., 1950.

"A Myth Unravels: Racism Didn't Kill Dr. Drew, After All," *The Miami Herald.* February 6, 1994.

Stern, Emma G. *Blood Brothers: Four Men of Science.*
New York: Knopf, 1959.

Who's Who in Colored America. 7th ed. New York: Christian E. Burckel & Associates, 1950.

Index

Boldfaced, italicized page numbers include picture references.